PANDORA'S GIFT

By

AJ BLANC

White-Knight Press

Copyright © 2025 by Andrew White

Library of Congress Control Number: 2025910110

Print ISBN   978-0-9994574-6-7
E-book ISBN   978-0-9994574-7-4

Written and published in the United States of America

Acknowledgements

Since writing is not my full-time job, I've had to concede some of my time dedicated to… what I'll call a hobby, for the essentials and other accoutrements that make up my life in recent years. It's not always easy to balance, even at the best of times. I have a great deal of respect and admiration for those who write for a living, because it can be a very trying experience. I once again would like to thank my friends and family for keeping me motivated when I was losing a little steam on occasion. I'd still be working on some of the basic elements of this forth book, so I appreciate your consistent encouragement.

My editor, Christel Hall, along with my freelance editor Robbie, has also helped me to further hone my skills, and to an extent theirs for finding so many details I missed. And due to being unable to connect with my previous cover artist, I'd like to welcome the excellent work by Radu Muresan at fiverr.com? I had a couple simple ideas for the cover and he brought them to life!

Dramatis Personae

Bredon Fitzroy: Defense Intelligence Agency Inspector

Divana Pris: Special Agent in Charge, Naval Criminal Investigative Service

Wray Corvo: Deputy Director, Naval Criminal Investigative Service

Harold "Hal" Dune, MD: Defense Intelligence Agency Investigator

Francis "Frank" Toolin: Special Agent, Bureau of Alcohol, Tobacco, and Firearms

Takashi Kimura: Special Agent, Naval Criminal Investigative Service

Juliette Van den Berg: Special Agent, Naval Criminal Investigative Service

Anessa (Anne) Kynes, Defense Intelligence Agency Supervisor

Arkady Mosin: Defense Intelligence Agency Program Supervisor

Steppan LeFleur: Detective, San Diego Sherriff's Office

Oskar Beaumont: Detective, San Diego Sherriff's Office

Harah Ibanez: San Diego County Chief Medical Examiner

Isabeau Fitzroy: Wife of Bredon Fitzroy

Elwin Koehl: Senior Engineer, Lockheed Martin

Akeylah Patel: National Reconnaissance Office Analyst

Glossary of Acronyms

ADP – Advanced Development Programs
BATFE – Bureau of Alcohol, Tobacco, Firearms and
        Explosives (appears as ATF)
CI – Confidential Informant
CID – Criminal Investigation Division
DIA – Defense Intelligence Agency (appears as "The
        Agency")
DISA – Defense Information Systems Agency
DOD – Department of Defense
EMP – Electromagnetic Pulse
EOD – Explosive Ordinance Disposal
ISIS – Iris Scanning and Identification System
LED – Light Emitting Diode
MARS – Military Asset and Repurposing Section
ME – Medical Examiner
NORAD – North American Aerospace Defense
NRO – National Reconnaissance Office
NCIS – Naval Criminal Investigative Service
ODIN – Orbital Defense and Intelligence Network
OSI – Office of Special Investigations
POD – Public Order Droid
SAC – Special Agent in Charge
SDI – Strategic Defense Initiative
SVR – Selective Variable Repeater
SWAT – Special Weapons and Tactics
TIM – Transponder with Isotropic Modulator
TSA – Transportation Security Administration
XO – Executive Officer (second in command)
WMD – Weapons of Mass Destruction

Prologue: Quiet Night

2082 – San Diego, California

How did it come to this? Bredon Fitzroy had always been careful. Never showing too much ambition in the places he worked. Tried to set a good example without imposing his opinions onto friends and colleagues. Always checking for loose ends and the usual traps people in his line of work fall prey to. Despite all his efforts, there he sat, bound to a replica antique Tiffany armchair by razor wire that was cutting into the flesh on his wrist and ruining the vintage leather.

"Let's start again," the raspy voice of his captor seethed. "Where did you put it?"

"Ugh, I already told you! If you're going to keep asking me questions I've already answered you might as well get this over with."

"Oh, am I boring you Fitzroy? Get over with what? I can do this all day."

"Hardly. Not when you keep checking the time every three minutes. This isn't my first tied-to-a chair experience you know."

"Perhaps not, but I'm willing to bet it's a first in your *own* safehouse. And your story about mailing it to Colony 426 isn't fooling anybody; our people see everything that goes through there, so let's cut the crap shall we?"

"Maybe your people aren't as good as you think they are," Bredon said, trying to obscure the doubts beginning to creep in. The other man responded with a knowing smile, sending a chill down the tortured man's spine.

"I'm not too worried about that. After all, *you're* the one who trained them. Didn't anyone ever tell you not to trust Greeks bearing gifts?"

Arkady. The realization hit him like a punch to the gut. He had never questioned Bredon's loyalty and determination before. The past few months however, he suddenly wanted to know every detail he could get his hands on. At first Bredon didn't think too much about it; Arkady did have clearance after all, it was just a strange change in behavior at a time when a new suspect seemed to emerge every other day.

"I see we're finally on the same page," Bredon's tormentor said smugly. "You're right about one thing though; my time here is short, so how about you show me a little of the respect I've given you by not resorting to… physical encouragement, like I was instructed to."

Bredon considered his options and came to only one conclusion. While the literal key to some of the more elusive successes in his life was hopefully still where he left it, hiding in plain sight, he didn't want to tempt fate and give this goon the satisfaction of knowing he'd been backed into a corner.

"The respect and candor are appreciated, even if it is coming from a blatherskite such as yourself."

"I'm sorry, a wha…" was all the man could get out before the house erupted into flames due to a flash of white-hot, ultraviolet radiation from dozens of burst transmitters hidden all over the house. From the outside, it appeared the residence spontaneously combusted. There was no telltale grey smoke emanating from under the roof to signify the signs of a slow burn. Nor was there the gradual growing of flames witnessed through the windows to alert someone of the imminent danger. No, this was an instant inferno brought on by a simple codeword uttered during a time of dire need.

Curious neighbors and other spectators flocked around the blaze, frequently checking whether or not the fire-suppression units in their homes were still active. With sirens wailing in the dark blanket of an otherwise quiet night, the full moon became eclipsed by the gathering smoke and bright flames that none of them would ever learn was the funeral pyre of a war hero.

Chapter One: Turncoat

Normally, approaching the main entrance to the Naval Criminal Investigative Service office filled Special Agent in Charge, Divana Pris, with a sense of pride; a feeling that has not diminished one bit in her dozen years with the agency. Today was different. This time, walking through the halls of the San Diego Field Office gave her a feeling of dread and resentment. Each step she took made her more anxious about the debate she was preparing to have.

Bredon Fitzroy was one of her training instructors at the Criminal Investigator Training Center in Glynco, Georgia. Not only was he an endless wealth of knowledge, he was also courteous to a fault, with a sense of humor that could make even the most serious of Marine veterans crack a smile on occasion; a description she fit at the time.

As fate would have it, Bredon would follow Divana to her first duty station in Florida after his term as an instructor had ended. They had not stayed in contact as closely as she liked when they went their separate ways, but practically all of the positive experiences during her formative years with the agency can be attributed to their working relationship. Reminiscing about those years made the news of learning Bredon had just died so close to where she lived and worked hurt that much more. That pain, however, would pale in comparison with what she was expecting from the meeting. She pulled all of the strings she had to have her office host the teleconference.

Divana shouldered her way through the conference room doors and plopped down into the nearest seat with a computer access station. She finally looked up to survey the room and noticed she was the first to arrive; one of the many habits her former mentor had instilled in her. "If you're not early you're late," Bredon would say at least once a week, along with "try to be first on scene for important matters. That way your information will be second hand at worst."

Her lapse into nostalgia prevented her from seeing two of her agents quietly enter the room and sit on the opposite end of the table. Perhaps they noticed her in deep thought and paid her the courtesy of not disturbing her. On the other hand, Divana found it more likely they were silent because they didn't know what the conference was about and were afraid to appear ignorant. She continued preparing for the meeting without addressing them, which they didn't seem to mind.

More agents and task force personnel steadily trickled in until all the local concerned parties were present. Divana knew most of them well; the rest only by name and reputation. As if on cue, all the projectors in the room lit up, interposing faces from the other side of the country where the government grey walls once were. Wray Corvo at headquarters in Quantico wasted no time with pleasantries.

"Who's carrying the bag with this one?" he asked in his light, tenor voice that contradicted his wide Polynesian frame.

"I am sir. Special Agent in Charge Divana Pris. I worked with former SAC Fitzroy for many years, starting at the academy then again at the Southeast Field Office."

"Copy that Pris. I'm sure you're not the only one present here who's worked with Fitzroy in one capacity or another, myself included. What do we know so far?"

"Focused explosion at a residence in Coronado, a few blocks away from the North Island Air Station. Damage was limited to only the one structure with two casualties inside: one confirmed to be Bredon Fitzroy, the other an unidentified male in his early-to-mid thirties," Divana said.

"How was Fitz identified?" Wray inquired, scrunching his formidable brow. "By the images I've seen the damage looked extensive. Stands to reason the bodies would be in a similar state."

Divana shifted in her seat. She knew the question was coming and wasn't ready to admit where her information came from. Luckily her source offered a few options to throw out as a temporary measure.

"His standard imbedded chip was too damaged, but he was still wearing his old service proteus watch. Given the location, EMTs assumed he was Navy and called local shore patrol, who then contacted us."

Deputy Director Corvo mulled those details over a moment before responding, squinting his eyes suspiciously in a manner others who had worked with him mimicked. "I get the sense that we're not hearing the whole story here, particularly due to the fact that you didn't really answer my question. Are you saying someone from your office identified him? I only ask because that seems unlikely considering his service predates current encryption protocol. Reading proteus watches would require special equipment that aren't normally carried into the field."

An uncomfortable silence followed, with all eyes on Divana to come up with a response. She searched her recent memory for one of the other suggestions recommended to her. Luckily, she was given somewhat of a reprieve from an unwanted source.

"Sorry to cut in while Pris pulls the foot out of her mouth, but so far there's been nothing presented here that puts this incident in our jurisdiction. Bredon Fitzroy's illustrious career with the agency ended years ago at his retirement, and according to my sources he was quickly picked up by the Defense Intelligence Agency as a contractor."

Valeria Sandor. The bean counter in DC. Divana knew she would be her biggest obstacle in convincing the agency to lead the investigation. With her intimidating particulars, Valeria gave her the opening Divana needed to make her case.

"That's correct ma'am," Divana said as her confidence level teetered on the edge. "Fitzroy was recruited by DIA approximately three years ago. Regardless, his service in the Navy and with us puts him at nearly forty years under NCIS jurisdiction. Combining that with him being a short distance away from Navy property, as well as a mentor to many currently in the service, I would like to formally request that we take the lead in this investigation."

A prolonged hush filled the conference room. The handful who were physically present exchanged nervous glances, too afraid to speak before those on the telepresence had a chance to. Just when the staring contest reached its limit did Wray Corvo crack a smile.

"You practiced that speech before the meeting, didn't you Pris?"

"I may have put a few words together sir," Divana conceded abashedly. "I'm trying hard not to sound like I'm begging, but I don't have to tell you that DIA isn't equipped to undertake criminal investigations… at least not homicides on this level of complexity."

"I'll plead the fifth on that subject," Corvo said. "Unfortunately, it's out of our hands I'm sorry to say."

Divana's heart sank. It was an outcome she was expecting; evidently she hadn't prepared for it adequately enough. "May I ask why?" she managed to get out through clenched teeth.

"Due to the sophisticated nature of the fire, and materials used to create it, this would fall under the Bureau of Alcohol, Tobacco, Firearms and Explosives purview," Valeria answered smugly.

"Except evidence shows that Bredon was restrained when he died, so the explosion was clearly a defensive tactic! The apparent torture and death of a government employee should be the focus here, not the account of the fire's origins. That situation isn't exactly ATF's bailiwick."

"I'd keep those comments to yourself Divana," Corvo shot back. "It may prevent them from accepting our assistance. Besides, in case you've forgotten, we go to the same training academy, so they are no less capable of conducting an investigation of this nature than we are."

Pris knew she had crossed a line by the Deputy Director's use of her first name. She could feel the case slipping from her grasp. Nevertheless, she had no intention of antagonizing Wray.

"I'll look forward to the possibility of turning my coat inside out to better blend in sir," she said, trying to disguise her sarcasm.

"That's more like it, sort of. We can do worse than Oliver Cromwell I suppose. Now then, I was just notified that someone has been dispatched to the scene. A Special Agent Francisco Toolin. Perhaps he would enjoy the personal touch of a face-to-face briefing."

It wasn't a question. Corvo had signed off leaving those not-so-subtle instructions loom over the conference room. Everyone else who had joined them remotely exited shortly thereafter, and a few support staff members physically present quietly departed. Divana dismissed the remainder to prepare to head to the scene so she could have a few minutes alone.

Once the door closed, she let out a sigh she had been holding in as she made a call on her mobile. A man in his late thirties answered, his auburn hair and hazel eyes practically glowing in the morning sun.

"How'd it go Prisca?" he asked in his reassuring voice, using the nickname he gave her when they met some twenty years ago, claiming it was the basis of her surname.

"About what we expected, aside from one big surprise; how could the ATF get assigned this and you not give me a heads-up about it, Dune?"

Doctor Harold Dune stared sheepishly back at her. "Yeah, sorry. Just found out myself. Even though Fitzroy was one of ours, he was apparently under investigation by them, for reasons I haven't been able to uncover yet. Everything and everyone around him have moved to a clearance level above mine all of a sudden. I can't perform a search without tipping someone off."

"Great. That's just great. Now I have to go play nice with the ATF in hopes of still being kept in the loop and I have nothing to barter with."

"Well, you have me, and your personal connection should count for something… right?"

"Some offense Dune, but you haven't exactly been a wealth of knowledge so far. And if Bredon was under investigation like you said, I'd be leery of anyone claiming a personal association with him if I were running the show. Can you at least tell me what he was working on before his records were sealed?"

"First of all, some taken. Secondly, from what I could gather he was a lead inspector for military equipment being released to other government and civilian markets, or logged for destruction. Lots of landmines involved with that no doubt; metaphorically speaking I'm sure."

"Oh, well, that's helpful… a little," Divana said. I'd like to keep this between us for now, as my ace in the hole for any future revelations if you don't mind. I'm off to meet with Agent Toolin. Message me on my secure line with any updates and I'll do the same."

"With unbridled praise like that, how could I refuse such an offer?" Hal said to a dead phone line.

Chapter Two: Quango

The unmarked NCIS vehicle pulled up unchallenged a block away from the still smoking house in Coronado. Due to the concentrated military presence in the area, flight by pedestrian and even government craft outside of an emergency was prohibited, so they had to get there the old-fashioned way; sticking to the streets and crossing the bridge against morning rush hour traffic.

As Divana's team of three approached, they could already see ATF evidence technicians swarming around the property like an organized bee hive. Collecting charred pieces, scrutinizing them through various tests, talking to neighbors and reviewing any available electronic surveillance footage. It all looked very methodical, which impressed and comforted her.

San Diego police officers were posted around the perimeter to control access and the media. The nearest officer took one look at the trio's matching NCIS jackets and badges clipped to their belts and promptly called over his shoulder to a man wearing an ATF polo shirt and baseball cap.

The man was average height and build, had tanned skin like someone from the Mediterranean, and a well-manicured beard. His movements were so fluid he seemingly floated over to them. The name Toolin was embroidered in gold, block lettering above his left breast pocket, but his most striking feature was his piercing blue eyes. Even under the shade of his hat they shown as if by their own light source.

"Morning. Special Agent Frank Toolin. I hope this isn't what it looks like."

"Happy to disappoint you, Frank. We're here to offer any assistance you might need. Special Agent Divana Pris, San Diego SAC. These are agents Takashi Kimura and Juliette Van den Berg.

"Pleasure," he said as he gave them a shifty look. "Was there any particular aid you were hoping to provide, or just being neighborly?"

"A bit of both," Divana answered after a few seconds of rumination. "As I'm sure you're aware, the identified body *was* one of ours for a long time. We also have some insight into the area that may be useful, considering we're surrounded by Navy property." She wanted to start firing questions at him right then and there, but resisted the urge for the time being.

"I see. So you're suggesting a quid pro quo between us then, because we landed the case instead of you?"

Divana cringed at the frankness of his verbal jab, then coughed away a laugh at her own pun with the man's first name. She sensed that Toolin was going to shut her down before she even had a chance, so she bit down her pride to stay in the game a little longer.

"You *could* say that. If I may be equally blunt…"

"Please do," Frank interjected in his timbre voice.

"Fitzroy was a distinguished agent and a personal mentor of mine. He's also a decorated Navy veteran, which I respect as a Marine. Some might argue that connection makes it a good thing I'm not running the case, so I'm asking, as a professional courtesy, to keep us on your shortlist of callbacks for any leads you may come across."

Toolin gave the three agents a hard look for a long moment while he considered the request. Eventually, he eased the tension with a mirthful grin. "I appreciate your honesty. Before I answer however, if our roles were reversed would *you* let someone from another agency tag along on a high-profile case?"

"Probably not, no," Divana replied quickly. "I would be resentful and distrustful of that person."

"Ah, so, now that you know where I land on that, or can at least empathize with it, what can you tell me about Bredon Fitzroy… without reading me his bio?"

Divana let slip a small laugh with that last comment. "Um, decorated Chief Petty Officer, accomplished NCIS agent both in the field and at the academy. Not what I would call a charismatic or prideful leader, but he was meticulous and would always try to get the full picture before acting. Retired a couple years ago to be recruited by Defense Intelligence shortly thereafter."

"That was… succinct. Any idea what he was doing here or who could've been with him?"

"Sorry, no. I didn't even know he lived here, only that he worked in what I like to call the 'tactical to practical' division."

"Oh, this isn't his house, not as far as I could tell anyway," Frank said. "He lives in Marathon, Florida with his wife of over thirty years. Lease is under the name of a William Karrde, with a K, out of Arlington, Virginia. That name mean anything to you?"

"N-no, I can't say that it does," Divana stammered. Damn you Hal, she thought. How could he not mention that Bredon didn't live there, or take the time to check herself? Saved by the bell, her watch chimed informing her of a new message on her secure line. To conceal her embarrassment, she excused herself to read the message in slightly more privacy.

"I can't help you with home ownership quite yet" she said, turning back to Agent Toolin. Although I do have a name for the other body in the house: Declan Quinn, also with DIA. Strange that one was bound to a chair and the other wasn't."

"What's stranger still is if that info came from the medical examiner, because I didn't get that message," Frank said. "Who was that?"

They stared at each other while Divana weighed her alternatives. She wanted to keep Hal's involvement to herself for the duration of the inquest. Then again, for the sake of cooperation that notion may not be possible.

"It's my contact in the DIA; an old friend from the war. He never knew Fitzroy, as far as I know, though he knew we crossed paths at NCIS and a little of our history."

"Uh huh, and what role does he play at Defense Intelligence?"

"Investigator, specializing in medical applications of military technologies," she added grudgingly.

"I can tell you didn't want to reveal those details. Now that you have, I'd like to chat with this contact of yours at his earliest convenience."

"I'll see what I can do," Divana said. "If he agrees, he'll likely prefer a face-to-face; he doesn't trust virtual platforms for off-the-record discussions."

"Fair enough. Just make it happen and I'll do my best to make room for you on the team."

"Is this an either-or scenario we're talking about here?" Divana asked, adding an edge to her voice she failed to suppress.

"It wasn't intended that way, but if you trust this guy his usefulness is as clear to me as it is you. There are just some precautions I need to take first."

"Such as whether or not he's involved in the ATF's investigation of Fitzroy?"

Frank Toolin offered her an impressed smile. "Well played. That, amongst other concerns everyone in our line of work has to worry about when dealing with outside intel."

The pair shook hands and Divana promptly spun on her heel and headed back to the NCIS van with the two other agents in tow. The short walk was irritatingly quiet, as Takashi and Juliette were tight-lipped throughout the trek back. Thinking about it, she didn't recall either one of them saying a word to her all day. Rather than let the tension fester, she decided to clear the air and came to a halt, sidestepping their inevitable collision if she hadn't done so.

"All right, let's have it. What's got you two so quiet today?"

They exchanged skittish glances, willing one to speak before the other. Eventually, Julie seemed to tire of their mental tug-of-war and became their reluctant representative.

"Nothing really, boss. It's obvious how close to this you are. We just wanted to give you your space."

"Besides," Takashi began as he was overcome by the urge to offer his brutally honest insights, "this isn't our case anyway. The most involvement we could hope for is a second-hand partnership. You seem to have an in with your DIA contact... which you didn't feel the need to tell us about by the way, so we propose you go find out what happened to your former SAC, and we'll work on some of our pending cases."

"With your approval of course," Julie added after a few beats of silence.

"Guys," Divana said with a sigh, "you know I don't have a filter, or an off switch. If you see me about to go off the rails from here on out, you are under instruction to call me on it. At any rate you're right, maybe it's best to keep your hands clean on this one.

Having said that, I'm not going on vacation or away on assignment or anything that might give you the impression you have carte blanche to do whatever you please. I still need regular progress reports, and authorizations haven't changed. Clear?"

"Clear," they answered in unison.

"Alright then, let's get back to base. I'll drive this time though; Julie's driving on the way over here almost put me to sleep."

~

Doctor Harold Dune's day was rapidly becoming complicated. The Defense Intelligence Agency was quick to claim Bredon Fitzroy was a casualty of an unfortunate incident, but for some reason they were keeping the identity of the other fire victim a closely guarded secret. He used every way he knew to cover his tracks digging up that piece of information; only time will tell if his efforts will pay off.

Hal had worked for the agency for close to a decade and he still felt like he was being kept at arm's length, getting only mid-level projects that no one else wanted. With his efforts on stopping, or at least significantly hindering, the illegal use of advanced synaptic implants (ASIs) finally showing progress, he was left sifting through the myriad of investigations that were unassigned or set aside for more senior agents. This may be his moment to shine through, he thought. His first major case since tying up the ASIs... assuming he could land it that is.

Presently, he waited in an old but lightly used formchair across the desk from his supervisor while she finished up a conference call. Anessa Kynes was new to the unit and was still getting to know everyone. Hal had heard rumors that she came from the Air Force's advanced research and development team, and seeing the plaques and shadow boxes around her office he could at least confirm she held the rank of major in that branch of service. The simulacrum of the holographic connection she was using vanished and she gave him a beleaguered look.

"I hate conference calls," she said with a gravity in her voice that startled Hal. "Especially when a simple message to everyone involved would suffice. Apparently, it's a weekly thing set up by Alun Longabaugh from downstairs. Maybe you can help solve this mystery; what is his job here exactly?"

Hal was caught off guard by the question and the confusion must've shown on his face because she smiled knowingly. "Sorry ma'am, I've been trying to figure that out for years."

"Guess I'll have to keep my ears open a little longer then. What can I do for you Harold? It is Harold, right?"

"Hal, please ma'am... or do you prefer sir?"

"I prefer Anne; Major at formal events, if we ever find ourselves at one. Sorry," she continued with a forlorn look on her face. "It's tough letting go of rank sometimes. There are days where I wish I was still in uniform."

Hal waited a moment for her to reminisce before continuing. "As do I, although the sensation isn't as fresh for me as it appears to be for you. This isn't exactly normal procedure but what I wanted to see you about is to formally request to be assigned the Fitzroy case... Major."

"Pulling rank on me already?" Anne said with a smile. "Technically speaking, there is no 'Fitzroy case.' That's a criminal investigation being handled by the ATF, or some such. For the sake of conversation, what is your interest in it?"

Hal took a deep breath to collect his thoughts before answering. He didn't want to tell her everything he knew, which wasn't much he had to admit, so he settled on the shotgun approach: throw a lot of data out and hope something hits.

"For starters, he died in a safehouse I set up. It's under one of my aliases and if whomever assigned to the inquest is any good at all it will lead right to me anyway..."

"So *you're* William Karrde? I see that name quite a lot. We'll have to talk about a few of those appearances another time. Please continue.

"Um, right. Secondly, while not an official part of the investigation, I know the SAC at the NCIS Field Office in San Diego; she was one of the Marines I ran around China with when I was a Navy Corpsman. She worked with Fitzroy for many years and is probably trying to schmooze her way into at least assisting the agent in charge right now. If she's successful in that venture, and I'm confident she will be, as she's very persistent that way, and we will have a direct connection to the investigation. With that, I can be a filter for this agency and potentially lessen any negative impact the inquest may create."

Kynes gave him a curious look, considering his words. "That's a well-thought-out answer, Hal. Did you come up with it on the fly or prepare a few bullet points beforehand?" She received a demurred smile in response. "Not important. What makes you think there could be a negative impact on the agency?"

"Well, given that Fitzroy was tied to a chair with wire, being interrogated by another one of our own, and that he set off the house's defensive system in a semi-affluent neighborhood, I think it's a logical conclusion that some heat may come our way... no pun intended."

"Good point," Anne said as she shifted in her high-backed seat uncomfortably. "However, I'm hesitant to give you the green light on this without first conferring with the man's chain-of-command..."

"I would prefer you didn't actually, in case someone in his unit is compromised."

"Oh? Don't tell me there's still more to this already complicated situation."

Hal gave her a hard look, trying not to reveal his clandestine activities he'd already engaged in with Pris. "Just being prudent. Don't want to make waves before even getting started."

"Alright. I'll hold off filling in Fitzroy's supervisor about the status of an employee he just lost in the field, for now. I can't stress enough that that arrangement has a limited shelf life; a few days at most. In exchange, I want every significant piece of intel you come across as soon as possible… and I'll be the judge on what I find significant, so err on the side of way too much information."

Hal sheepishly thanked her and departed the office as quickly as possible. He walked right past his desk and headed for his National brand company car. He knew Anne wasn't playing around so he needed to meet with Pris right away. Little did he know that she was already keen to set up a meet and greet with the ATF investigator.

Chapter Three: Tempest

Frank Toolin was directed to a recently vacated corner table in the open-air bar of Kettner Exchange. The upscale restaurant sat on the edge of the largest Little Italy in America, and quickly became one of his favorite places during his short time at the San Diego Field Division. It's classy, vintage-looking décor reminded him of his previous duty station in Chicago, which even after ten months he was still somewhat homesick over. Fortunately, days like today helped to make him get over that particular ailment.

It was late October, yet he sat practically outside drinking a cold beverage and wearing a short-sleeved shirt. Autumn was his favorite time of year, and while he was missing the changing leaves and shift to natural colors, he was enjoying not wearing jackets or sweaters yet. Now that he thought about it, the necessary change in wardrobe may not come; rumor was San Diego had only one season.

He spotted Special Agent Pris making her way around the tree growing in the middle of the rooftop bar and stood up to make his presence known. In tow with her was a man about his height, perhaps slightly taller, with thick auburn hair, wearing a similarly colored mackintosh jacket. If he didn't know any better, he could swear he'd seen this image in an old noir film.

"Special Agent Frank Toolin, this is Investigator Harold Dune of Defense Intelligence," Divana said somewhat gruffly. Frank could tell they were familiar with each other, yet they had the air about them as if they had just been arguing about something. They all sat and Divana busied herself with the menu projected above a side table. Frank didn't want to get in the middle of what was going on between them, but his time was somewhat short after already spending the time to get here from Coronado.

"I'm getting nothing from the crime scene, so perhaps you could shed some light on a few things, Dr. Dune. You *are* the same man from the Omnium fiasco about nine years ago, right?"

Hal sighed. "They told me that would be 'need to know' only!"

"I remembered your name from a report indirectly related to the incident, from the San Francisco Police Department if memory serves. Don't worry, your secret identity is safe with me," Frank said.

"You take down one multi-billion-dollar company and suddenly everyone thinks you're a movie star," Pris mumbled derisively.

"Um, three actually, but you wouldn't know about those other two," Hal stated proudly. Turning back to Frank he said "what was your interest in the case to begin with? It didn't have an ATF connection as far as I know."

"An Army buddy of mine living near San Francisco got accepted into one of their vocational programs. He had an issue finding and keeping work, even though he was the most gifted person with languages and codes I ever met. That was the last I heard from him. Once I learned Omnium was going through a complete restructuring, with federal charges hanging over their head, I tapped into a few state-controlled databases when I moved out here."

"It's a fine line between being famous and infamous, isn't it?" Divana asked with an attitude she couldn't seem to shake.

"Not when any fame directed at *you* should be attributed to someone else," Hal shot back. "A police inspector died while trying to escape their Tahoe labs."

A somber moment followed, with Hal and Divana eyeing each other angrily. Frank thought it a good idea to break the standoff so discussion could get moving again. "Do you two need to get a room or something?"

The death stares he received caused him to slink down into his seat as far as he possibly could to escape them. What he perceived as sexual tension was now a much more preferable concept to the present development.

"No, Special Agent Toolin, we do *not*," Divana seethed. "Our respective spouses may not appreciate that very much, and one of us wouldn't survive the encounter," she added back to Hal.

"Just a simple, uh… difference of opinion before we came up here," Hal said. "Now then, shall we get down to business?"

"Fine by me," Frank said with a sigh of relief. "How about we start with where you found the identity of the other body at the house? The medical examiner had barely started her examination."

"I didn't really," Hal admitted. "I came across some chatter about a man missing from our extraterrestrial division and did some digging…"

"I'm sorry, your *what* division? You mean like ET?" Frank asked.

"That's right. The term literally means 'outside Earth.' I know the NCIS and DIA has offices in the colonies; I'm sure the ATF does as well."

"Oh we do, to a lesser extent I'm sure. It's just not called that."

"Tomáto, tomàto. Anyway, I found that despite his job, Decland Quinn's assigned duty station was a lot closer to where we're sitting, which made no sense because the ETs serve no function in this part of the state. That's when I noticed his duty assignment had been retroactively changed the day before, by someone with managerial access."

Frank stared at Hal, expecting more information. When none came, he looked to Pris who simply shrugged. The reason for their 'difference of opinion' soon became clear.

"I hope there's more to that story and you were just pausing for effect, because in my experience that's what we call… nothing."

Divana stifled a laugh, which Hal pretended not to notice. "As it happens yes, there is more. I was debating whether or not I should reveal this right away, but after I was granted permission to look into Fitzroy a couple hours ago, I pinged his chip location, along with others in the vicinity, right before the bomb went off. I went this route because a ping wouldn't tip off anyone else who may be watching this investigation. The results show Decland Quinn's position as 1.6 meters away from Bredon Fitzroy up to the point both of their implants went dark, at approximately 21:21 hours last night."

Both of them stared at him agape. Hal couldn't help letting a haughty look broach his face. "Why didn't you tell me this sooner?" Divana asked, her raised voice attracting onlookers from across the bar.

"You didn't give me a chance to. You were too busy reminding me what I *didn't* do. Besides, that was only confirming something I already suspected. The real shocker was learning Fitzroy wasn't actually under investigation by the ATF; he was an informant."

This time all eyes fell on Frank. He shifted uncomfortably on the maroon leather cushion, the ice melting in his empty glass suddenly becoming more interesting. "Where did you get that information?" was all he could muster without meeting their eyes.

"This true Toolin?" Divana asked. The veneer of annoyance from a moment ago was whisked away instantly by this new development. "From what I understand, the DIA doesn't generally handle weapons and explosive materials, so what could Fitzroy possibly inform you about?"

"They may not be physically around them on a regular basis but access is pretty much carte blanche, especially their records and contracts. There were... whispers of arms being diverted from their destinations during shipping. Not big caches; a crate here, an item there. The frequency however was often enough for somebody outside the circle to notice. Normally, the Agency would be responsible for investigating such matters and according to Bredon they were not only taking no action, certain members were pressuring him to not look into it at all. He saw no other option than to seek help elsewhere. That's where I came in. He was my CI. I transferred from Chicago *specifically* because Fitzroy convinced me everything was culminating here, so when he's found dead in a DIA safehouse tied to a chair, with another agent present, I'm left wondering who I can trust."

Hal and Divana sat solemnly while they considered the implications of Frank's words. Suspecting someone within the Department of Defense of murder was already an uphill battle, adding conspiracy into the mix made things much more complicated.

"Don't take this the wrong way," Divana said gently, "but why you? Are you a specialist in this sort of thing or something?"

"I asked for the case when a buddy of mine I went to the academy with tipped me off that some of the equipment was... misappropriated from my old stomping ground of Fort Campbell. I dreaded thinking about what someone could do with the kind of tech the Airborne use on a regular basis."

"Screaming Eagles huh? Nice. I'm former Force Recon, and the good doctor here was our corpsman for a while."

Frank smiled and visibly relaxed some. "Sounds like I'm in good company then. What say we get down to business, wha... the hell is going on down there?"

All three rose to the sound of multiple car alarms going off. The walls were too high for safety reasons, but there was the occasional window to peer out of, and all three crammed into the closest one in their corner of the rooftop bar. From their vantage point they could see a wayward Public Order Droid; though they often went by another name in most places.

"That snitch bot down there is bumping into all the cars," Hal said stating the obvious. "Must be malfunctioning."

"Snitch bot? You want to uh... elaborate a bit more on that?" Frank asked, completely dumfounded.

"You didn't have those in Chicago? Anyway, they're officially called public order droids. You can see the POD number on the top of the dome there," Divana said, pointing at its bucket-like top as it continued to crash into the same vehicle.

"The term 'snitch bot' was coined in Singapore I believe, where they were first deployed, and the name stuck," Hal said. "Basically, they roam around town watching and listening, and alert the police if they come across anything illegal."

"I've been here almost a year and I don't think I've ever seen one."

"You probably have and didn't realize it. Most are painted to blend in to whichever area they're assigned. Actually, I thought they were all camouflaged in some way; strange this one isn't. It seems to *really* like that car too."

"Damn, that's my g-ride," Frank said. "That thing has already dented it!"

"Your government vehicle is a Bollinger?" Divana asked admiringly. "How did you swing that?"

"Somebody somewhere succeeded in the age-old argument that government vehicles are often cheap and repair heavy. Paying a little more for better quality equals less funding spent on upkeep and all that. I better get down there and stop that thing lest that rare success comes to a screeching halt."

Frank departed in a hurry and Divana plopped into her seat with a sigh. Hal continued to stare, stunned at the snitch bot's behavior. Why had it hit every car on that side of the block to abruptly stop at Toolin's unmarked vehicle, he wondered.

"Shouldn't we call somebody about that POD?"

"Like who, the PD?" Divana said. "I'd say it's a matter for the city's tech department, or possibly the local manufacturer's office. All the cops could do is tell us there's one here, and we already know that."

"Okay, you take one, I'll contact the other. That thing is acting *way* too suspiciously for a simple error."

"How so?"

"Let me count the ways. First there's the…"

Hal was cut off by a massive explosion from behind, throwing him practically into Divana's lap. Both were disoriented due to the concussive blast, but it didn't take them long to realize that the explosion had come from the street.

They rushed over to the now pulverized window and gasped at the scene below. The spot where Frank's car and the snitch bot used to be was now a smoldering crater. From their vantage point it appeared the Kettner Exchange was still relatively intact, however several cars had been blown completely across the street.

"Oh my God, Frank…" Divana breathed, barely able to put the words together.

"I can't be here," Hal said.

"What? Do you have a concussion or are you just in shock?"

"No I… well, maybe I do. I mean I can't be seen here with you, working on this case. If you still need my help, and I'm to retain my autonomy, I need to leave, now."

Pris contorted her face in anger to give him a dressing down he'd never seen before, then she saw the logic in his words. Even though it had only been a few hours, an attack on Frank felt like an attack on her as well. She didn't want to put Hal in those same crosshairs if she could help it.

"Alright. We'll head down to assist and you can duck out when you see an opportunity. But be ready to jump when I get done here. The gloves are coming off if Toolin was caught in that blast. I hope we're on the same page here."

"We are. You knew that before you asked," Hal said firmly.

They hurried down the stairs to the first floor, ushering the other rooftop patrons and staff along with them. The restaurant's exit was on the side opposite the explosion, facing a small parking lot, where a growing group of people had gathered. They had neither seen Frank in passing nor outside and assumed the worst. A cacophony of sirens from seemingly every direction was descending upon the scene, which gave Hal his opening to perform his disappearing act.

Divana scanned the cluster of confused and terrified faces. She tried to think of something reassuring or uplifting to say but felt just as disorientated as they all looked. Instead of taking charge of a scene like she normally does, she decided to blend into the crowd like the other witnesses.

Chapter Four: Bloodlines

Hal's journey out of town was wrought with trepidation. He was still shaken up from the explosion, and every time he tried to calm down an emergency vehicle would zoom by overhead, or a billboard would show news of the bomb site, collapsing his composure.

He had no intention of returning to the local DIA office; not until he had to. There was this feeling in the back of his mind that he was being watched. Perhaps it was just paranoia, but the possibility of that bomb being meant for him as well as Toolin was growing stronger in his mind the more he thought about it. Due to this insecurity, he made his way to the only other place nearby where he felt safe, apart from his home: the Marine Corps base at Camp Pendleton, where his wife was stationed.

Established in 1942; the same year its namesake, General Joseph Pendleton passed away, Camp Pendleton was the west coast's premier Marine training facility. There was such a wide variety of divisions and training commands represented at the Camp that Hal doubted he knew half of what went on at its 125,000+ acres. Despite his many visits, and carrying a high enough security clearance to get him into nearly every area of the expansive base, the extent of his knowledge there still only scratched the surface.

His destination this time, as it usually was on base, were the offices of the 1st Marine Special Operations Battalion. Lieutenant Colonel Lindsey Dune was now second in command of two divisions of that battalion, which was about the limit of information she was willing to provide on her daily routines. Hal had reminded her on many occasions that his security clearance was actually higher than hers, yet she aptly pointed out that just because he *can* have access to her records and operations, doesn't mean he has a *need* to know.

He parked his dark grey, National brand government vehicle in the only space marked 'visitor' and sat a moment collecting his thoughts. The shaking in his hands had subsided, but his pulse was still racing. Times like these always reminded him about his son, Sean.

Hal was terrified of being a father. When Lindsey told him she was pregnant, he remembered stammering through multiple conversations about the subject, which often ended with him in a cold sweat. With everything he had seen and done in his life, caring for another person from birth seemed like an impossible task. Lindsey was as solid as a rock throughout her entire pregnancy, and stayed at work until almost the day Sean was born. Hal was a wreck though, and hesitated when the time came to head to the hospital.

All that apprehension seemed to evaporate the first time Hal held his son in his arms. The whole world paused just for a moment, and holding onto that moment was his go-to method to get through tough times. While Sean wasn't as keen on being held by his father much anymore, now that he was close to turning fifteen, Hal will always have that day in the hospital.

He climbed the stone steps to the building that housed Special Operations, and realized what an unremarkable and obvious government building it really was. Being a Navy veteran and federal employee, he was used to architectural styles that were more for pragmatism than inspired design. Yet it still surprised him, even for such an old base, how forgettable so many buildings are. Although it was heresy for a sailor to admit, Army bases were often a more pleasant experience.

Hal weaved his way around the virtually identical hallways and shouldered his way through the heavy wooden doors of the Special Operations Battalion. From there he proceeded to enter the row of offices for commissioned staff and was met by a locked door. Confused, he looked around for a button or something that would allow him access, but all he found was a smug-looking corporal behind a high desk.

"Can I help you sir?" the Marine asked in a bored monotone.

"How long has this door been here?" Hal responded, still somewhat befuddled.

"It's always been there sir. Perhaps the difference this time is a lack of escort… or maybe an appointment?"

Hal turned slowly to fully regard the young man and saw someone who most definitely didn't want to be there. His grooming and uniform standards were impeccable, as those guidelines were drilled into every Marine very early in their service. His posture and body language told a different story altogether. Shoulders and core were slacked, sitting back a bit too comfortably in the barstool-like chair, yet his attitude was borderline confrontational.

"In my day, we actually *stood* watch, if you catch my meaning corporal."

"Well sir, rest assured that watch standing hasn't changed since 'your day.' I would be standing if I wasn't on light duty due to an injury. Then again, I probably wouldn't be here at all."

"I see," Hal said sheepishly. "Please forgive me."

"All will be forgiven once you tell me what your business here is."

"Oh, yes. I'm here to see Lieutenant Colonel Dune. And you're right, I don't have an appointment."

"Well, the Colonel is in the middle of an op briefing sir. She may not be available to see you."

Hal wracked his brain over what operations were going on that Lindsey might be involved with. He was confident it wouldn't be something she'd tell him about, so that narrowed it down to three possibilities. Rather than making it known that he was there for a conjugal visit, he thought it best to aim for a more occupational-oriented approach.

"Uh, yes. The situation at the consulate in Parime City, Mars. That's why I'm here... from Defense Intelligence."

The young man eyed him dubiously for a long while, then asked for Hal's identification. He visibly relaxed after confirming Hal's claim, and a semblance of a grin broached his face.

"Very well sir. I'll call Lieutenant Prax to escort you. Are you armed?"

"Yes, I am actually. Is that a problem?"

"No sir. Not for somebody with your credentials. I just need to record as many details as possible regarding civilian visitors to this building. What are you packing?"

"The SVR-10 with standard police ammunition, or so they say," Hal said.

"Ah, the selective-variable repeater. We call those the M77. Do you know why that is?"

"I'm familiar with the military designation but no, I don't know the history behind it."

"From what I've read, when we were doing its field testing somebody called it the Star Wars gun. When it was adopted into service it became the M77... for 1977."

Hal mulled that revelation over a moment, as well as pictured the weapon in his head for comparison. "Interesting, but it doesn't really look like anything from Star Wars that comes to mind. It's a little similar to the Bryar pistol, though not all that closely."

"A man of culture I see! I thought the same thing, almost exactly. The lieutenant will be along shortly to take you to the colonel. Thank you for your patience."

Hal considered sitting down, figuring it would take his escort a while to arrive. No sooner had the notion crossed his mind than the door burst open with an officer calling his name and directing him inside. She looked equally young to the enlisted man at the desk, though she carried herself with a poise that defied her perceived age.

"So, Lieutenant Prax, is it? What role do you get to play around here?"

She glanced at him briefly without breaking stride, giving Hal a look that instantly made him feel like he had crossed a line with her.

"I'm Colonel Dune's aide-de-camp. She hasn't mentioned me... Inspector Dune, is it?"

"Inspector is fine, but I prefer Hal. I'm afraid neither of us talk about our work much outside of our respective offices. She may have said your name at some point and it slipped my mind, sorry."

"Think nothing of it," she said curtly, though Hal could tell it bothered her that she wasn't a regular topic for discussion between him and Lindsey.

They passed through a small, tastefully furnished outer office to knock on an unmarked door. Despite there being no windows, there were several healthy-looking plants and colorful pieces of art to brighten the place up. His wife's voice granted them entrance after a brief pause, and Prax hardly opened the door fast enough for them to go inside.

"Inspector Dune to see you ma'am."

"Thank you, Harah. If there's any more of that coffee left, can we get two cups? If not don't worry about it, we'll manage without."

The lieutenant curtsied and departed as quickly as she arrived. Hal sat on a plush chaise lounge with a sigh and made himself comfortable. "She's eager to please. Almost cried when I said I didn't know who she was."

"Inspector? When did that happen?" Hal shrugged in reply. "For your information, she specifically requested this assignment when she graduated top of her class at Annapolis. She really keeps me on my toes."

"No offense to either of you, but wouldn't this job slow her career down? A high-flyer like that could be working at the Pentagon, or any one of our foreign bases. She'd give you a run for your money in no time."

"I've had this exact same conversation with her, and do you know what she said? That she wanted to work for a woman who served with her father. Her father was enlisted under my command and died defending Taiwan," Lindsey said with a pang of guilt.

"Well, that probably narrowed it down quite a bit."

"Not as much as you might think."

There was a knock at the door and Lieutenant Prax came in with a tray of coffee and all its accoutrements.

"Thank you again Harah. I'm sorry I didn't do this before; this is my husband, Hal. We met when he was with NCIS; he's since moved to Defense Intelligence. You two have something in common: you're both working under your means."

Prax looked at Hal, then to Lindsey, then back at Hal again, betraying nothing in her demeanor.

"In my case," Hal said, "she's probably referring to the fact that I have a doctorate but don't do anything related to it. I could only guess how that may be compared to you."

"I'm quite content with where I am, thank you," she said firmly and departed without meeting their eyes.

"That settles that I guess," Hal said glibly. "Still a better attitude than the guy working the front desk though. He certainly isn't content with where he is."

"Is this why you came here? To criticize my staff?"

"No, I actually came here to hide. There was an explosion downtown that I was witness to and I thought it best to lay low to avoid having my name on a police report."

"What!? Downtown where? Was anybody hurt?"

"I was meeting some people at Kettner and somebody attached a bomb to a snitch bot. An ATF

Agent I was meeting with was caught in the blast. Others could be hurt too, but he's most likely DOA."

"Geez. And here I was going to tell you to get lost because it's not a good time for me right now. Still isn't. I can simply ignore you if duty calls; I've gotten pretty good at that over the years."

"Oh that reminds me, how is the situation in Parime City by the way?" Hal asked with a grin.

Lindsey shot him a disappointed look. "I suppose I shouldn't be surprised you know about that, but don't change the subject. How well did you know this agent who you think died?"

"Not well. It was our first meeting. The get-together was also arranged by someone you might recognize; Divana Pris?"

"Oh wow, Pris!" Lindsey said with genuine surprise. "She's one of the many people we both served with. What's she up to these days?"

"She's the Special Agent in Charge for the NCIS Field Office in San Diego."

"That sounds like a good fit for her, though she probably finds being the boss dull. I won't waste my time asking you what case you're working on together, still, please give her my regards. She was one of those Marines I never had to explain anything to. I could ask her to do something, even if she'd never done it before, and she would figure it out."

"She definitely likes the challenge of unique problems," Hal added.

"Exactly! She had three older brothers if I remember correctly, so she's immune to machoism. A self-motivator who was dependable to a fault and didn't need micromanaged. Wish we had more like her."

"That's apparently a similar description to the man whose death I'm investigating," Hal revealed reluctantly.

"So now you're a homicide detective?" Lindsey retorted.

"No thank you. He was one of ours with the agency. Died in a safehouse I arranged for traveling agents and foreign counterparts. ATF was assigned because he was suspected of weapons smuggling, by the division of the DIA responsible for disposing of them."

Lindsey regarded him for a moment. "That's the most you've ever talked about a case, while it was still active anyway. This one must really be bothering you."

"Bothering? No, I'm *terrified*. Two people with a close connection to me have died and I don't yet know the extent of this thing. It's not even an official investigation; too afraid to step on someone's toes… or to be implicated. I don't feel safe anywhere."

Another few beats of silence passed between them. Lindsey was about to try and reassure him when a chime sounded demanding her attention. "I'm sorry, I have to take this. Try not to do anything distracting."

While she talked business on what he assumed was a direct link to their troubled colony on Mars, Hal weighed his options and didn't like what he saw. Tip toeing around was getting him nowhere slow. He needed to take a hard look at what Fitzroy was up to the weeks before his death, however he couldn't do that without official authorization from up the chain, or without putting a bullseye on his back. He was trapped in a state of circular reasoning that only he could break out of.

Hal rose and mimed that he was going to leave. When he reached the door Lindsey muted her conversation and stood over the projected simulacrum to get his attention.

"Sorry I couldn't be of more help, but you're rarely one to play by the rules. Go do what you do best and kick down a few doors. Oh, and please don't give the corporal out front a hard time. He was injured trying out for Force Recon, as his past two generations had been part of. Although he'll probably get another chance, in his mind he has ruined a family legacy."

Hal nodded and thanked her. On his way back to the car his head swam with what his legacy might become. If he had anything to say about it, he vowed to not make it one of lost opportunities.

Chapter Five: Bulletproof

The scene outside Kettner Exchange was still a madhouse when Divana Pris finally left. She lost track of how many people she gave a statement to; police and firefighters all asking her the same questions and not answering any of hers.

She walked back to her cruiser in a daze, thinking over everything that had happened and hoping that through sheer willpower she could force it all to make at least *some* sense. Her dismay was so deep she was reaching for the door handle before she realized somebody was standing next to her car.

He was tall and wiry, with thinning grey hair and piercing grey eyes to match. Pris would say the man looked like a vampire, except for his severely weathered face and mangled right hand. At a glance he appeared to be missing a finger and a half, along with some scarred flesh from a burn that will never fully heal.

"Pardon my forwardness Special Agent Pris, but this is a matter of a… delicate nature."

"Sorry friend," Divana said, "I don't do delicate, especially after the last couple hours I've had."

"Ah, yes. I empathize with your frustrations. Bomb investigations are very draining. I've had to deal with them as well; too often I'm afraid."

"One of them a little too close for comfort?" Divana asked as she bowed toward his gnarly hand.

The man lifted his right hand up to inspect it as if seeing it for the first time. "You could say that. No matter the amount of training and experience you may have, there's always the possibility of surprises. Now then, I understand you have a vested interest in seeing that the death of Bredon Fitzroy is investigated to a satisfying conclusion?"

She gave the man a hard look for several seconds before answering. "That depends on who's asking, and equally important, *why* they're asking."

"Of course. My name is Arkady Mosin, Program Supervisor with the Defense Intelligence Agency. Bredon Fitzroy was one of my specialists. I hadn't worked with him before, but he had quickly lived up to his reputation of being smart and reliable. The *why* I'm asking is simple: let our own investigators handle this. Your personal connection is laudable; this is an internal matter."

"If it's so important to keep things in house, how did another agency take the lead on the investigation mere hours after Fitzroy's death?"

"That was out of our hands, for reasons I'm sure you're aware of by now. Since that side of the investigation appears to have ended, we prefer to proceed unencumbered. The Agency will no doubt send memos to the ATF and NCIS. I wanted to inform you personally."

Divana suddenly felt the hairs on the back of her neck stand up and had the urge to pull her weapon. "That sounds like a threat, on an armed federal agent, with the remains of the prior investigator scattered barely a block away."

Arkady put up his hands defensively. "No threat intended Agent Pris. Only a respectful request to let us take it from here. There are circumstances here you don't yet fully understand."

"That's the whole point of an investigation, to find out what happened and why, typically collaborating with others to reach an efficient resolution. If you already have these answers, perhaps you would kindly tell me so I can consider the case closed?"

"I wish I could, but we're no further along than the ATF was. Our own investigators are seeking the same answers and need the time and freedom to do so. Conversely, even if I did have that information, I would be bound by confidentiality to share with you."

"Actually, our rules are the same. We're both employees of the Defense Department, so there'd be no conflict in sharing notes. How about we start with what Decland Quinn's role was with your agency?"

A look of alarm flashed over Arkady's face, which was quickly replaced by the emotionless mask he'd maintained during the remainder of the conversation. "I suppose it shouldn't be surprising you know that name. Since he seems to also be a victim of yesterday's fire, I see no harm in telling you that he is… or should I say was, part of our Foreign Liaison Unit. Before you ask, that unit operates almost exclusively out of DC, so I have no idea what he was doing here."

"I can tell you what he *wasn't* doing; sitting down for a nice cup of tea with Fitzroy," she shot back sardonically. "And I heard he was part of the extraterrestrial division or something. Who or what does this unit liaise with exactly?"

Another brief glimpse of surprise from Mosin. "The ET div is a part of the foreign unit. They coordinate with foreign military officials, both here and in the colonies, for the exchange of data, equipment, and occasionally personnel…"

"Weapons? Would some of the 'equipment' they deal with happen to be weapons?"

"It wouldn't be out of the ordinary if they were, Agent Pris. The US government deals in millions of dollars in arms so often it would shock most people. Nevertheless, I couldn't say for sure what Quinn's role with us was; he isn't someone I work with and I've never met nor spoken to him."

"I see, good to know. So, what exactly do *you* do at DIA?"

"I supervise the Military Assets and Repurposing Section, or MARS. It goes by other names; perhaps you've heard one or two of them. I prefer to highlight the Roman mythology connection, since that's where the acronym was derived from.

Ultimately though it's one part of DIA's Inspection Unit."

"That's all very interesting but I'm looking for the connection between…"

"I'm going to have to interject here and conclude this before you get the impression I'm trying to be helpful. I've made my appeal, with a more formal one to the NCIS to follow shortly. If you can restrain yourself and abide by this request, I will personally share our findings with you. Good day Agent Pris."

With that, Arkady Mosin entered an unmarked yet obvious government vehicle that seemed to materialize across the street. Divana was certain it wasn't there when she approached her own vehicle, and the tint job on the windows were too extensive to see inside. She got the distinct feeling that it was self-driving and used some sort of camouflage to appear as a more unassuming car.

She finally settled in her own cruiser and immediately dictated a message. "Hal, we need another face-to-face A-SAP. You're not going to like this, but meet me at the base in time for happy hour. I have to report in and I get the feeling I'll be dying of thirst shortly thereafter, if you catch my meaning."

She sent the message to his secure line, then took a few deep breaths to stem the flow of adrenaline making its way into her system by Mosin's perceived threat. Mentally preparing oneself for a firefight can take its toll on the body, and Divana had honed what she learned long ago to minimize that affect. After what seemed like several minutes, though in fact had been less than one, she set her auto-navigator for the NCIS office on Welles Street and began to prepare herself for another daunting experience; conferring with the boss.

~

Hal was waived through the entry gate 32 on Yama Street at Naval Base San Diego, or NBSD. He wasn't sure why he decided to enter the base through one of the less frequented gates, but somehow it comforted him not to be passing through the main entrance at the moment. Despite there being only one lane of traffic in each direction, with the end of the civilian workday in full swing the exit traffic was far busier than his direction. This particular entrance was also the farthest from where Pris arranged to meet, allowing him to drive around seemingly lost to see if he was being tailed. He eventually concluded he was in the clear and pulled into the base's oldest public bar.

Dying of Thirst, or the DOT to the locals, is the city's second location, and was a place where enlisted, commissioned, and civilians could drink together in relative harmony, as opposed to the officer's club down the road. The place used to be called the Budweiser Brewhouse, but that company lost its contract several decades prior due to some downsizing across the nation. Although it wasn't as busy as it would be on a weekend, the parking lot was still filling up fast.

Hal narrowly made it past security and paused to scan the dim interior for Divana. Either the DOT had remodeled since last he'd been there, or his memory of the place was skewed by drink. Almost half of the bar area had been transformed into a classy, pub-style setting with high-backed chairs and as much faux cherrywood as could be squeezed in. There was still room for large sporting event crowds, and the outdoor beer garden enjoyed a permanent structure to protect its patrons from the few elements San Diego threw at them. This new place looked like one Hal could easily become a regular in, if he wasn't always traveling for the agency.

He spotted Pris as far away from the door as possible, yet still visible, and she made no indication she had seen him. Once a Marine always a Marine, Hal thought. If it can be helped, never put yourself in a situation of disadvantage, and don't give away your position. He ordered whatever was on tap by the Coronado Brewing Company from the happy hour menu and made his way to the back booth. Pris's attention was split between the door and her folding tablet.

"What's good here?" he asked, knowing all too well that she was a buffalo wings aficionado.

"Your guess is as good as mine," she retorted. "I already polished off a dozen wings wondering if you got my oh-so-subtle message; they're not as good as I remember. What kept you?"

"Am I late? Happy hour isn't just an hour in most places you know," he said defensively as his beer was plopped down on the table. "At least the service hasn't changed here. Anyway, I was taking a leisurely drive back from Pendelton trying to look out for tails."

Divana stopped what she was doing and squinted at him despite the low light. "You have a government vehicle, right? They wouldn't have to tail you, the thing's probably filled with trackers."

That realization made Hal want to bang his head on the table. Instead of giving her the satisfaction of being right, he said "want to keep the skills sharp where I can." She just nodded and let a smug grin broach her normally neutral façade.

"I don't think the Agency is following you yet anyway… at least that's not the vibe I got from my little chat with Arkady Mosin." She briefly covered her meeting with Fitzroy's shady boss. If any of it surprised or worried Hal he didn't show it.

"Seems like the actions of a man desperate to keep something hidden," he eventually said while placing two orders of pulled pork nachos.

"You mean like gun running and selling military equipment? Yeah, but it was more than that. He was practically begging me, like someone had run over his dog and he wanted me to put it out of its misery."

"How many drinks did you have before I got here?" Hal asked warily. "If that's the best analogy you could come up with you should probably be cut off."

"Sorry. I just kinda wanted to kill his dog after that ambush of a conversation."

"Um, ok. Do we have another alternative, in case he doesn't have a dog?"

"Since the well is starting to run dry on my end, how about you make a little more noise on yours? I have to imagine an audit of Fitzroy's cases needs to be done. If that's being handled by that Mosin guy the argument could be made how that might create a conflict of interest. So how about you insist on starting that argument?"

The food Hal ordered arrived and he asked for another round of beers. After the server left earshot, he said something that shocked Divana. "Yeah, ok. Let's try that."

"Uh, what? I'm sorry, that was the last thing I expected you to say."

"You think you're the only person who can stick their neck out? We have the same things at stake here: family, job, reputation…"

"Don't forget life," she added.

"Right. Well, that's not all on you. If there's something rotten in the state of Denmark, it may take an insider to clean house anyway."

"Macbeth?"

"Hamlet."

"Damn. I always get those two confused. Try not to show too much disappointment."

"No deal," said Hal. "That does give me an idea though. Perhaps this thing is more than about money. An unhealthy dose of ambition was Macbeth's undoing, speaking of. What little we know points to something bigger than simple greed."

"What little we know? We know practically nothing! We can't even say with any certainty that

Defense Intelligence is doing anything wrong… other than being completely uncooperative in a joint investigation. I probably would be too in their shoes, all things considered."

"We're not as bad off as all that. On my way back to the city it occurred to me that since the safehouse's security features are voice operated, or some of them anyway, it would be constantly recording once a voice is detected. I'm sort of pro tem landlord of the building that burned down, so I have access to the security system via the cloud. I checked and we have audio and some video of the whole evening."

Divana sat motionless for several seconds staring at Hal, deciding whether or not to strangle him. She opted not to for the moment without completely dismissing the idea.

"Next time, lead with that please! Can you send that recording to my secure mobile?"

"Wow, the P-word. I would say I'm honored to hear that but I know when you use it it's more of a threat than a request," Hal said before finishing off his pile of nachos. "I didn't download anything, in case that's logged or can be discovered in court, though I did run it through a transcription app a friend from the US Marshals recommended while playing it out loud. Here's what it spit out."

Hal forwarded a copy of the transcript to her flex tablet and she read it multiple times in total silence. Hal knew her well enough to see she was getting angrier with each read-through. When she'd had enough, she let the tablet thud dully on the tabletop.

"For a little while, maybe a few minutes at least, I was considering taking a backseat, to let you do more of the heavy lifting. Now I don't think I can. Tell me you know what it is they're looking for."

"I don't, but I have a theory. While not impossible, it isn't very likely Fitzroy simply stumbled across evidence of arms dealing, otherwise he'd probably have done more about it than tip off the ATF. So, given his time with Naval Intelligence, and his variety of experience at the NCIS, I think he got his hands on an infinity key."

Divana stared at him dimly until she finally realized he wasn't going to elaborate without prompting. She did so in her usual manner by throwing her hands up in an animated shrug.

"Oh, sorry. An infinity key is pretty much what it sounds like; a key that opens practically anything… I'm talking digital locks by the way, if my theory is correct. Since the Chinese manufactured a sizable amount of our electronics before the war, we didn't have great success cracking their encryptions. With the help from some of our allies like Japan and Germany, strangely enough, we were able to turn that around toward the end."

"Ironic that. So when in your theory do you suppose Bredon procured this infinity key?"

"Twenty years ago, give or take, when he was with intel. The unredacted parts of his service record says he spent time in several allied nations of the

Pacific Rim, particularly Singapore. It all fits within his timeline."

"And you think a two-decade old piece of tech would still work?" Divana asked dubiously.

"On our systems, if Singapore is where he got it from? Definitely. We may have upgraded software a dozen or so times since then, but we still use the same general operating system."

"Ok, well, I suppose it's somewhere to start. Do you happen to have any other *theories*, because I have to say this one feels pretty thin to me."

"I do, but they have even less to go on. If that changes, you'll be the first to know."

"Great, now you have me curious as to what else is banging around in that head of yours. I'll keep myself in suspense until…"

"What is it? You trailed off a little there," Hal said.

"You might want to head home. There's an emergency recall at my office and I don't want you anywhere nearby if it's connected to what we're talking about."

"Don't have to tell me twice. Keep me posted."

Chapter Six: Insurrection

Divana Pris dashed over to the NCIS building a few blocks away from Dying of Thirst. She wasn't out of shape but her footwear wasn't built for prolonged jogging, and her feet were already sore from the casual walk to the bar. Might need to get rid of these shoes, she concluded.

The entrance to the building came into view and she could see two uniformed figures guarding the doors with the telltale sleeve of shore patrolman, so she slowed her pace to appear more dignified, when in actuality it was to find some reprieve from her shoes.

"What's happened?" she asked as they took turns scrutinizing her credentials both physically and on a small, handheld reader. After what took far longer than it should have, they simultaneously nodded to each other in the affirmative like automatons.

"Not sure ma'am. Something about a breach. Don't know the variety," they answered one after the other as if they rehearsed it. Divana cocked her head and they stepped aside to allow her passage.

The hallways seemed eerily quiet. All the offices she checked were empty with the lights still on, despite it being after regular working hours. One room after another she saw partially full cups and water bottles, chairs left askew, and purses and gym bags still sitting where they were haphazardly tossed after lunch. By all appearances it seemed the people who normally made the office buzz with activity vanished in the middle of their daily routines. It wasn't until she approached the conference room that she started to hear familiar voices.

She burst into the conference room expecting to have all her questions answered by mere sight alone. Instead, what she saw was even more puzzling. Her staff all sat around the conference table while two men in black suits stood at the head of the table like they were giving a presentation. All the normally friendly faces carried a look somewhere between respite and uncertainty.

"Ah, good, Special Agent in Charge Pris. We were just about to begin without you," the one on the left said. If they were to swap places in the blink of an eye Divana would have difficulty telling them apart. They looked so similar they could be brothers, yet she didn't think they were. Same height, same slicked back dark hair, same steel-blue eyes. Despite all that she was willing to bet they had been surgically altered to look that way.

"Who are you and what are you doing here?" she demanded, throwing all diplomacy out the window.

"Very well," guy on the left continued. "I'm Agent Johnson, this is Agent Jonston. We're here from the Defense Information Systems Agency because we've detected a breach in your data inventory management system and have come to investigate."

For several long moments nobody said a word or even moved. Divana figured they wouldn't give her any more details than that, but she liked to think the silence made them uncomfortable.

"Yeah, couple things about that. One: DISA doesn't have any agents. It's an agency of analysts and programmers who track down the lowest bidders on software for the Defense Department. Two: our system operates on a national platform, so if there was a breach, other offices would be affected as well and my phone would be blowing up with messages. How about you cut the crap and tell us what you really want so we can all go home."

Divana was bluffing a little on both points; she didn't know exactly how her agency's network functioned. She felt it was close enough to reality and wanted to gauge their reaction to her challenge. When their response came it was practiced and swift.

The mute one on the right reached into his sport jacket on the opposite side to extract a long-barreled C81 machine pistol and began firing wildly around the room.

Bullets peppered the walls from the weapon's wide spread. Divana, sensing the movement as hostile, dove and rolled under the lip of the large conference table, all while trying to bark orders over the weapons fire and warnings from the other man in black.

"Agent Pris," the man on the left calmly said. "We know you're armed, as are some of your colleagues here. However, nobody has been hurt so if you'll cooperate we'll be on our way as quickly as possible with that unchanged."

They were in somewhat of a stalemate. If she gave into their demands they could kill them all anyway. If she did nothing that would likely speed up the same process. The psycho duo definitely had the upper hand, so Divana had to think quickly to exploit any edge she could. Gasps and wails began to break out amongst her staff, which told her decision-making time was over, and then movement under the table sparked an idea.

"Ok," Divana said loud enough to hear over the commotion. "I'm coming out. Don't shoot me!" She counted to three before taking aim through the diamond-shaped holes along the wide table leg and firing at the knee of who she hoped was the man on the right.

Divana knew she hit her target by the surprised grunt and wasted no time with the confusion she created. She rolled to the left of the table and ended in a kneel. The man with the machine pistol was in clear distress, though not so much as to not notice her and aimed his weapon at her a second time.

In an age where body armor can be hidden in most garments and still be effective, particularly in an untailored business suit, armed conflict sometimes becomes even more complicated than it already was. Knowing this, Divana put two more caseless rounds into the gunman's head, then quickly trained her weapon on the assumed leader of the two as he reached for his own concealed weapon.

"I wouldn't if I were you," she warned. "Your twin there doesn't need any company just yet."

The remaining man in black glared at her but didn't remove his hand from inside his jacket. Divana was afraid to blink as the seconds stretched on and tension began building in her shoulders. After several breathless moments the edge in his stare relented enough for her to become hopeful their deadlock was about to come to a close. Then the doors to the conference room swung open and one of the shore patrolmen from outside stormed in with his sidearm drawn like a one-man SWAT team.

"Nobody move! You there, get your hands out where I can see them."

The warning returned the grim determination to the stranger's eyes, as if an additional opponent gave him the challenge he was hoping for. His weapon came out faster than humanly possible. The jittery shore patrolman began to unload on him with complete disregard to the office staff seated around the table. Divana's agents and support personnel tried to slink down in their seats more than they already were.

Despite the barrage of gunfire, the man in black managed to land a few shots on the officer, causing him to retreat back into the hallway. That just left him and Divana, and she had no intention of retreating, namely because she had no cover that didn't endanger someone else. The man was wavering visibly; clearly injured from the exchange seconds ago, but she didn't want to risk trying to apprehend him and sent the same treatment she did his partner: two bullets to the head. He dropped like a marionette with its strings cut.

"Kimura, check their vitals. Van den Berg, collect their weapons and empty their pockets onto the table. The rest of you, please gather by the door. Take your seats if you like," Divana barked to secure the scene as quickly as possible before base police swarmed the building.

"Mind if we hit the head boss?" one of her investigative analysts asked, already halfway out the door.

"Go for it. But come right back and don't make any calls or send any messages yet."

Everyone not already engaged rushed out of the room like it was on fire, bumping past the still stationary shore patrolman.

"You alright there chief? Might want to call this in if you haven't already, then start interviewing witnesses so we can get out of here sometime today," Divana advised before turning to her agents rummaging through the mystery men's garments. "Find anything useful?"

"You mean other than these two being practically twins, right down to their pocket contents?" Juliette Van den Berg said. "What do you suppose *that's* all about?"

"They're spies," Takashi Kimura answered. "The softened facial features, no distinguishing bodily marks; forgettable with only vague description details.

You could put one of these guys on physical surveillance and not know which one is which at a given moment. The question is who do they work for and what are they doing here?"

"That's two questions Kashi," Julie jibbed. His response was a sardonic smirk.

"I have a pretty good idea," Divana cut in, "only a couple agencies have the funding for this level of clandestine operation… in America anyway. Get whatever identifying information we can before the bodies become off-limits. I'm willing to bet this will get sourced out to San Diego PD. I know someone in the medical examiner's office; I'll give her a heads-up, maybe we can stay in the loop."

"Why wouldn't base police let us handle it?" Kimura asked somewhat defensively. "Last I checked there were a few investigators here at the Navy's disposal.

"Yeah, and some of us are even good at it," Julie quipped.

"You just answered your own question," Divana interjected once more. "If this happened somewhere else on base we wouldn't be having this conversation. It wouldn't look kosher if we investigated the shooting of two people in our own office; two people who had a legitimate reason to be here by all appearances. Besides, our base hospital may have a morgue but it's not equipped to do a forensic examination. The PD might be a better choice in this situation; they're less likely to be swayed by government pressure."

~

Hal deployed his landing struts and touched down on his driveway in Carlsbad; his wife Lindsey's childhood home. She came from a long line of Marines who somehow ended up at or near Camp Pendleton toward the end of their career, so the house had been passed down through the generations.

He stared at the house, with its deceivingly welcoming outside lights, that will turn bright and angry on anyone its facial recognition software doesn't know, and considered the likelihood that those legacies may end with Lindsey. Their son Sean, now 13 as of a few weeks ago, hadn't shown interest of any kind in the military, and they weren't going to push him. A lot can change in the intervening years between now and when he comes of age, and those will be exciting years to behold.

As if he'd been reading his mind, Sean appeared at the front door gesturing Hal to come inside. Gone are the days when he would run full speed into his dad, knocking the wind out him in the process, nearly every time he came home. Hal was gratified Sean still acknowledges his return, though he's uncertain whether he misses the enthusiastic greeting, or is relieved that his abdomen is spared the impact.

"Somebody's here to see you dad," he yelled over the whine of the hydraulic motor lowering the car to its resting position. The message made Hal stop in his tracks and sent a chill down his spine. He scanned the street and noticed an older-model government vehicle; even older than his National Astral. He silently berated himself for not noticing before, and gave Sean a quizzical look for more information.

"She said she's your boss," he volunteered. Hal relaxed some with this news, although it raised more questions than answers. Why was Anne Kynes at his home... assuming it was indeed her? Keeping a neutral façade, he bounded up the couple steps to where his son was standing and tousled his hair before embracing him.

"Hello to you too Sean. It's formal dress for this event I see," Hal said awadmiring his son's wardrobe. Sean looked down at his wrinkled cargo shorts and tee-shirt featuring an anime character Hal didn't remember the name of. Sean's response was a shrug and a smile. They entered the foyer and friendly chit-chat could be heard coming from the kitchen. Hal thought it an appropriate moment to announce himself in grandiose fashion.

"Honey, I'm home!"

"In the kitchen... weirdo," Lindsey retorted.

He strolled in to see them sitting at their small pub table next to a bay window, where he and Lindsey sometimes have breakfast together. Relief seeped into his psyche a bit more seeing that it was Anne, however his joke to Sean now felt out of place because she was wearing a striking, silvery cocktail dress.

"Why do I suddenly feel underdressed and *way* too sober?" Hal noticed there was an open bottle of chardonnay with two full glasses, neither of which appear to have been touched.

"You're in luck then," Lindsey said, "you can have my glass. I will take the rest of the bottle elsewhere so I can resist eavesdropping." She got up and headed for their ground floor bedroom, patting him on the shoulder as she passed. Hal watched her go, then reluctantly turned to regard Anne.

"I told her she could stay; nothing confidential about this visit," she said sounding somewhat anxious.

"We don't talk much shop at home. Too many secrets, in both of our jobs. Too much opportunity to blur the lines if anything were to come under review."

"So she said. I don't recall approving overtime for… whatever it is you've been working on."

Hal gave her a confused look as he picked up Lindsey's wine glass. "I *hope* you know what I'm working on, since you gave me the verbal go ahead this morning."

"Yes, about that… I've been keeping an ear out, to make sure you've been following my instructions, and while you haven't been implicated explicitly, I don't like what I'm hearing."

"I don't think I understand. I've kept the office's hands clean of this. What have you heard?"

"This started out quietly looking into the death of two DIA employees; no problems so far. Then I learn the ATF agent assigned to the investigation dies in an explosion, which very much looks like a hit, mere hours after we chatted. That made me a little nervous for your safety. Had you been there…"

"I *was* there," Hal interjected. "Slipped out before emergency services arrived. We were comparing notes on Bredon Fitzroy."

"Well, that's just terrific," Anne said exasperatedly. "Don't tell me anything, yet. Anyway, after news of the explosion came to my attention I started poking around about Fitzroy, and was almost immediately slapped down by DIA Security saying his file was now 'need to know' only. That was a serious red flag for me. With two of our own dead you'd think they'd want all hands on deck."

"This is very close to the argument I presented to you this morning. What's changed that you felt the need to come here ready for Cinderella's ball?"

"Oh, why thank you. I think I could give Cinderella a run for her money in this," Anne said as she admired herself. "What changed is now every resource that could help resolve this has been cut out. To solidify my suspicions, I just learned there was a shootout at the local NCIS office, involving the very agent pushing to investigate Fitzroy's murder in the first place."

"What!? Was anybody hurt? Are we taking point on that?"

"Take it easy. By some miracle, only the two infiltrators were killed, but reports have been vague and infrequent getting to me so far."

"Ok, what are we doing about it?"

"Officially? Nothing. Local yokels will be investigating the shooting. While they're busy with that I want you to get to the bottom of this, whatever it takes. The reason I'm dressed like this is because I decided to strategically move up my mandatory supervisor training, so I can have plausible deniability if your actions turn out to be fruitless, or illegal. To help, I've sent you my access codes; use them wisely or they'll lock us both out."

"That sounds like an easy way to set me up," Hal said with growing apprehension.

"You may not need them at all; it'll be your call. I'm sorry to cut and run on you like this but you know the agency better than I do, and your reputation for exposing corruption should make the right people nervous… if that's what's going on here."

"Well, I suppose this is better than you ordering me off the case and I keep doing it anyway. So what's with the dress then?"

"It's for a party at Vandenberg that I'm on my way to; part of the alibi so, don't tell anybody I was here."

"Will do… or won't. Bring me back something nice from your trip, I'll try to do the same."

Chapter Seven: Redress

There's something to be said about people who can approach each day as an opportunity to improve on the last. Bredon Fitzroy was one of those people. He didn't dwell on what he could've done differently the day, even the hour before. He held himself accountable for his actions and moved on after they were done.

Divana Pris wasn't like that. She didn't often second-guess herself, though she did try to picture what might've happened if other choices were made. Scenarios ran through her mind considering different outcomes by changing her actions in a fraction of what it took in real time. Occasionally her luck changed for the better, but those were by far the exceptions. Some have called her a perfectionist, for good reason. She likes to call it being pragmatic.

This was the reason she felt like a zombie, even after a more rigorous morning workout than usual. She had spent half the night replaying the conference room shooting in her mind, and every alteration she made resulted in the death of either herself or one of her staff members. So what was her problem then? All her people got to go home, with a few requesting some leave, yet who the two men were and what they really wanted still remained a mystery.

That was how she spent most of the other half of the evening; researching whatever came to mind. Who would need to utilize such deep cover assets, and who could deploy them at a moment's notice? At first her immediate thought was the Defense Intelligence Agency, but she soon counted them out as lacking the viability for such an endeavor. While the Director of National Intelligence website did contain a list of members within the intelligence community, it wasn't detailed enough to narrow down her search.

It wasn't in Divana's nature to make decisions based on gut feelings; she preferred to have at least *some* factual basis before following a line of inquiry. Desperate times called for desperate measures however. The Central Intelligence Agency was the most likely candidate but, like the DIA, they didn't need to send spies to retrieve something from within the Department of Defense; they could simply ask or force the issue in a number of legitimate ways. There were a few agencies working very closely with the CIA that may want to gain some attention for themselves. Of those on that list the NRO seemed the most likely candidate for a boost into notoriety.

The National Reconnaissance Office has been in a custody battle since nearly its establishment in 1961. While the NRO is still managed by the Defense Department, it's primarily operated by the CIA, which has been slowly increasing their hold with more personnel and operations there for decades.

Considering that the NRO has dominion over the country's network of military and reconnaissance satellites, from design of the orbiters themselves to their management, they are in a perfect position as purveyors of real time information to be selective in how and when they disseminate that data.

To help her focus her mind, Divana had taken up yoga in recent years. Nothing particularly challenging yet, just a short morning session alone in her spare room where she threw down a mat that matched her clay-colored carpeting. At first, she was somewhat self-conscious about it; seemed strange to her that a Marine was doing yoga. She soon got past that upon feeling the physical and mental benefits even a light routine offered.

Today the topic on her mind was Hal's theory about Fitzroy having an infinity key, and who would gain most from obtaining one. The way it was described made it sound useful to almost anybody, so that wouldn't lead her anywhere. Instead, she decided to focus on how other people would suspect him of hacking and it hit her. Divana quickly finished out her session, then dressed and messaged Hal to meet her at the Broken Yolk Café.

~

Are we always going to meet 'clandestinely' at places where food is served?" Hal asked as he slid down into the blue and white vinyl bench seat. Although it was still early, the popular restaurant near the airport was starting to fill up with hungry tourists and locals alike.

"Shut up. Listen. I don't suppose we could get access to Bredon's computer, could we? Desktop or tablet?"

Hal shook his head. "Whatever he used in the field would've either been taken by the people who tied him up or burned in the fire. His desktop wouldn't be much help either, since his office is on the other side of the country."

"Right. Which brings me to plan B. I might be able to find someone to get into his office. Until then, would his travel itineraries be considered top secret or could anybody check his calendar?"

"Might be wrong but I don't think that's something you can just turn off until several months after separation," said Hal. "I can check right now. What am I looking for?"

"What was he doing here? His job was to oversee appropriation or destruction of military equipment, or some such, right? So he was likely here for that purpose, and my guess is he was either following the people he suspected were stealing military hardware, or meeting with Toolin. I have to imagine he'd been tracking this pattern of thefts for a while."

"Makes sense," he said. "Here we go. I was expecting an additional layer of password protection but I guess if they did it for him they'd have to do it for everyone who isn't in secret services."

Hal turned his folding tablet so they could both examine Fitzroy's calendar. A pattern to his travel became immediately apparent.

"Every two weeks, like clockwork," Divana said. "Not a very secretive pattern. Do these locations mean anything to you?"

Hal turned the tablet to be able to read it more clearly. He entered in a few commands to overlay a map with the locations highlighted and dates visited. "At a glance, I'd say most of these coincide with Air Force bases, with a few Marine bases sprinkled in for good measure."

"That's a neat trick. I don't think either of those branches are represented in Indianapolis though. Do you have another guess? He visited Indy quite a few times. Almost every third trip he took."

"There's an Air Force Reserve base in Grissom, not far to the north from there. I'm sure they stockpile loads of retired equipment waiting for destruction or a new home in the private sector." Hal grimaced in thought for a moment before continuing. "I also seem to recall a chemical weapons and explosives depot in Newport, Indiana. That was Army ran however and shut down decades ago. Let's hope that's still true."

"Ok, so that would fit your theory," said Divana. "But if he was going there for DIA business, why wouldn't he fly there directly? You guys are authorized to use military transport, right?"

"Authorized, yes. Generally welcome to take advantage of those transports, no. I don't have to tell you about the rivalry between branches of service. It's far worse with contractors. Even civilian members of the DOD get the cold shoulder a lot of the time, except on the occasions we're doing something positive for the base or commander. Besides, if he was following a lead he'd probably want to keep a low profile."

Pris conceded that point, although she felt she was still missing something. "Ok then, assuming you're right, why *these* bases? What makes them so significant to cause one of the lead inspectors to travel so frequently, potentially into harm's way each time?"

Hal returned to scrutinizing the map of bases, making notes as he went along. After a few agonizingly long minutes Divana could swear she saw a light bulb appear above his head.

"Ok," he said, enunciating each letter. "A little over half of the Air Force bases have, or at least had, either atomic weapons or controlled materials to use them. As I'm sure you know, the Air Force manages two-thirds of our nuclear arsenal, with the Navy in control of the rest. Most of the other USAF locations seem to be either related to Space Force or National Reconnaissance Office, or both."

"The NRO? I thought they were independent, only managed by the DOD. Why have they set up shop in so many Air Force bases?"

'Well, it stands to reason that there's satellite offices outside their headquarters in Chantilly, Virginia. And it would make sense to have those offices at least near military property, since they use their equipment more than anybody else. My question is, what's the link between the NRO and Space Force?"

"Not to mention the Marine bases and Fitzroy's reason for being here," Divana added.

They ordered and ate, neither speaking for the duration. A few times it appeared Hal was about to say something, only to then fill the void with another bite of his croissant avocado egg and cheese sandwich. Divana rarely spoke while eating. At a young age, her grandmother drilled into her to not mix talking and eating because "you end up doing neither very well" she would say. Every time Divana disobeyed that sage advice she could hear her gram's voice in her head and felt instantly guilty. She dearly missed the woman who raised her as much as her mother more often than usual during those times.

At Hal's second cup of bitter, diner coffee he had an epiphany, and set the once white melamine mug down too clumsily, causing a brown patch to grow across the as yet unused napkin. "I think I've pieced it together. This might be trying to fit a square peg in a round hole but it explains almost everything." Pris waited patiently for his dramatic pause.

"The Marine bases were early on in the... campaign let's call it, so those were to secure some conventional weapons, in case they needed them. Then they went around trying to collect items related to atomic weapons, and when they couldn't find them went to Grissom to test their luck there. Finally, the NRO controls our satellites, right? Adding all that together leads me to the conclusion that they, whomever 'they' are, are building their own nuclear football," he finished with a sigh. Divana just stared.

"Nuclear football as in the briefcase-thing handcuffed to some guy who travels around with the president? Isn't all that's in there a codebook, some procedures for the president to follow, and a way to communicate with the right people should the need arise when outside a command post? Seems like a lot of work to make a radio only one person can use at a time. And where does the infinity key enter into this story?"

"It's traditionally a satchel actually, not a briefcase. And they wouldn't need access to the entire arsenal," Hal said, already regretting his brainstorming efforts. "Could simply be control over one site, or even the satellite network that the football connects to, which is part of the reason infinity keys were devised in the first place; breaking satellite encryption."

"That's plausible, I suppose," Divana said as she paid the bill with a wave of her hand over the matte black scanner in the center of the table. Hal slurped down the rest of his coffee and they headed toward the parking lot.

"Pretty sure I've said another version of this before but we need to start turning some of this science fiction into fact. I'm not convinced…"

They were dressed like police trying very hard not to look it. The tall one leaning against her car had close-cropped hair and beard, and wore shoes that looked more expensive than all her pairs combined. The other one was pudgier yet could probably handle himself well if he needed to. His tan sport jacket was quality work, though it's lack of proper tailoring gave off the vibe of a lucky thrift store find rather than its wearer being the original owner.

"I think one of us has the wrong car," she said, moving her hands to her hips, close to the handle of her sidearm. The tall one stood up, offering her a mirthless smile in response.

"Detectives Steppan LeFleur and Oskar Beaumont, San Diego Sherrif's Office."

"French heritage?" Hal asked.

"Cajun," the big one named Oskar snapped. They both gave Hal a hard look for several seconds, then LaFleur softened some.

"Special Agent Pris? We've come to collect you to attend the postmortem for yesterday's... incident."

"I don't like the sound of that," said Divana. "How did you know where I was?"

"Rang your office. An Agent... Kimura I believe it was, said you sometimes like to come here to prepare for a day where you may not get the time to eat."

Damn that little blabbermouth! Outwardly she expressed nothing, internally she made a mental note to explain the finer points of discretion to Takashi at her earliest convenience.

She said "That's good detective work. Unfortunately, I have my own contact with the ME's office and I haven't heard a peep from there about being ready."

The odd couple hesitated, exchanging furtive glances. A pause suspicious enough to prompt Hal to draw his SVR-10 pistol. All three of the others were frozen where they stood, dumbfounded by the sudden escalation.

"Easy there big man," Steppan said in a scoffing tone. "I don't think we've been formally introduced. Would you like to see my credentials, or are you offended you didn't get the invite to attend the autopsy?"

"That depends on your explanation of Agent Pris's quandary," Hal said. Everyone waited for him to elaborate but none came.

"Her 'quandary' being why I'm passing along this information instead of Dr. Ibanez, who I assume is her contact? I haven't the first damn clue. When was the last time either of you checked your messages? Or, alternatively, she decided to follow procedure and give the investigating agency first crack at how to proceed."

Hal considered both points and regretted needlessly drawing attention to the situation to passersby. Regardless, he wasn't going to back down until their intentions were verified to his satisfaction. Too many people have died the last couple days and he had yet to learn why. He glanced over to Pris with his peripheral vision and noticed she was on her mobile, frantically looking for something. The adrenaline coursing through his body was causing his hand to shake a little, and a slight itching sensation in his fingers. Thankfully Pris intervened in the impromptu standoff.

"Looks like I got the notification from the ME's office about twenty minutes ago. I suppose you're off the hook for that. Still doesn't explain why you came to 'collect me' instead of calling."

Steppan shrugged his wide shoulders and said "I'm a hands-on type of guy. Shall we?"

"You don't really think I'm getting in the car with you, do you?"

"Guess not. Follow me closely then; I'll get you into the employee parking lot. Is your quick-draw friend here going to be a plus one, so he doesn't feel snubbed?"

"No," said Hal, putting his gun away as slowly as possible. "I have a POST Academy class to teach about providing professional courtesy to people from other law enforcement agencies."

"Aw man! I just finished a class that was a waste of time. I gotta take another one now?" Oskar said, not quite grasping the sarcasm. Steppan glared at him then gestured to get into their unmarked police cruiser.

"Find me some science-fact," Divana said as she approached her own vehicle, leaving Hal wondering if he should follow, to prevent her from adding two more bodies to her repertoire.

Chapter Eight: Cold, Hard Truth

The city's primary morgue on Overland Avenue was obscenely secure, Divana Pris thought. They had to pass through two car checkpoints, and an armed private security officer solely to gain entrance to the building. Once inside, another contracted security guard took their fingerprints electronically and confiscated their weapons and electronics.

"You said we were going to the morgue, not Donovan Correctional," Divana jibed as they were ushered through the double doors of the security station. The room was a perfect cube with reinforced walls that blocked cell signal, and had cameras pointing in every direction so there were no blank spots. On the positive side though it had excellent acoustics if someone got the urge to sing or play music.

Steppan turned and said "What did you expect? They don't let just anybody in here to contaminate biological evidence. This is an accredited facility; we have a reputation to uphold."

"Yeah, except you don't need four layers of expensive private security contractors to protect it either. That's double the checkpoints than at your average military base, and you don't hear about a whole lot of breaches there."

"That's reassuring," he continued. "I doubt there's a military in the world that's forthcoming with their trespasser history. And when the public do hear about an infringement, it's usually a very serious one, so you get what you pay for."

Divana made no rebuttal. He was right of course, but she wasn't going to give him the satisfaction of saying so, especially in light of what she's been chasing her tail over for the last couple of days.

The chill from the autopsy theater could be felt outside the pressurized door in the clean room. They donned the disposable gown and mask, as required to enter or risk a permanent ban to the facility, and Oskar pressed the button to slide the metal door open with a quiet hiss.

Dr. Harah Ibanez turned and made a drawn-out gesture to look at her watch, a move that might've landed better had she actually been wearing one. The point was still made however. Her jet-black hair was pinned up in a tight bun, and the layers of surgical garb hid the fact she was once an Olympic athlete.

"If I'd known you'd take this long I could've been almost done by now," she said to the detectives.

"We went to collect her on the way," Steppan bowed toward Divana. "She took some convincing, with great personal risk to ourselves."

"I see. Special Agent Pris, I understand these two guests are your handiwork?"

"That's right," answered Divana. "It was a lose-lose situation. What have you found so far?"

"Before I answer, you should know your access to this inquest will be limited, considering you're likely under investigation by the Sheriff's Office and your own agency. These two gentlemen are here to keep me honest in that regard."

"That's funny doc, I thought it was the other way around," Oskar said sporting a sly grin. Harah shrugged and turned to two large wall displays that had data scrolling by like a stock ticker.

"Now that that's out of the way, my external examination has revealed a lot of strange anomalies which tell us very little about their identities… by design I suspect. Other than the bullet wounds, any potential identifying features have been removed: birthmarks, moles, et cetera. Their friction ridges, both hands and feet, have been altered to appear identical yet still retain friction skin. Their teeth are also identical, despite the fact they are clearly not twins. Their hair is the most realistic synthetic fibers I've ever seen, yet not real hair. In fact, all their natural body hair has been removed, including eyebrows and nose hair."

"Jesus doc," Oskar said, "who would put themselves through all that?"

"I can only speculate on that. I presume these are the callsigns of deep cover operatives. What I don't understand is why two American spies would try to infiltrate an NCIS office?"

"So they are Americans then?" Divana asked, not sure she needed that information.

"Oh yes, almost certainly. We'll know more after we've completed the examination, but based on their bone density gleaned by x-rays, I'd wager they were both from the Midwest. Not the same place I don't think. Good money is on the general region of Kansas, Missouri, and Oklahoma. I'm getting ahead of myself though. The next *external* anomaly I wanted to point out are the eyes; they aren't theirs. More specifically, each man has one natural eye, most likely Asian in origin, and one cybernetic eye."

"Cybernetic?" said Steppan, stepping out from the corner he was hiding in for the first time since they entered the autopsy theater. "We might be able to trace the manufacturer, and possibly even the purchaser since usually only the government and very rich can afford those."

"My thoughts exactly," Harah said. "I was preparing to scan their eyes when you arrived." She and her diener wheeled over the ISIS machine, or iris scanning and identification system, which was already close at hand. "We normally check both eyes at the same time but in this instance, we'll start with the natural eye."

Specula were attached to keep the eyes open and a bright light was projected from the ISIS. The machine made a soft ping sound when the scan completed, extinguishing the white light.

"As I feared," Harah said, "this eye was transplanted from an Asian. A deceased one at that. Shiwan Badal of Lucknow. Reported death nearly six years ago."

"Begging your pardon Doc," said Oskar, "that name sounds Indian to me. I thought you said the eye was from an Asian?" The other four people in the theater stared at him a moment before Harah chose a more diplomatic response.

"Quite right Detective, that is indeed an Indian name. For categorizing purposes however, according to state and federal regulations the term Asian includes people from the subcontinent of India, Sri Lanka, and Bangladesh. Now, moving on to the other eye."

The scanning light lit up the opposite side of the dead man's face. After a few seconds, the light changed from white to blue, and then red shortly thereafter.

"I've never seen that happen before," the diener said, and then an alarm began to sound.

"Everyone out!" Harah yelled as she tugged on the arm of her assistant. "That's the radiation alarm!"

Divana turned to get Steppan moving but he was already out the door. His partner on the other hand was transfixed onto what was happening to the body. Harah slapped him on the shoulder and that was enough to break his concentration and get him moving.

With everyone herded into the cleanroom, Harah smacked the emergency decontamination button to seal them in and perform a series of air and surface cleaning procedures. While that went on, Oskar watched in amazement as the body they had been examining melted due to a series of nodes overheating with delta radiation. Steppan took one glance through the small window and promptly vomited.

"Really?" Divana said. "We don't have enough to worry about as it is?" He was about to respond when a loud pop came from the theater, followed by a plunge into complete darkness and silence.

"What the hell?" someone asked; Divana couldn't make out who. After about a full minute dim emergency lighting glowed to life, followed by the return of the radiation alarm shortly thereafter.

Harrah nudged Oskar a step to the side to gain access to the door's small window. She gasped upon seeing the condition of the body. "Any idea what that popping noise was?"

Oskar turned and with a deadpan expression said "the guy's head blew up. Pretty sure it was his mechanical eye that did it, after the rest of his body turned to goo."

"Then it must've also been the source of that electromagnetic pulse we just experienced," said Divana. "The timing between the two couldn't be a coincidence."

"Somebody really doesn't want these guys identified," Steppan said hunched in the corner.

"You should stand up if you're still feeling queasy Detective," Harah warned. Steppan eyed her with a look that began as annoyed, then transitioned to one of embarrassment.

"Thank you, Doctor, but I'll be fine. Actually, I see no reason for us to still be here. The autopsy is probably on hold until a hazmat team comes by, and then maybe bomb squad for the other guy's eye. That's a day, at least, and you should limit who's in the room with you when you get back to business, just in case. Am I right?"

Harah pursed her lips, pondering the man's words for a brief moment. "That's an accurate assessment of the situation. We'll still need all of your statements about what happened."

"Fair enough. You know how to reach us." Steppan said as he rose to leave.

"Wait," Divana interjected. "We can't just leave. Aren't we all potentially irradiated? Aren't we supposed to be cleared by… somebody?"

"While you probably *should* be checked before you go, the advantage to delta radiation, if you want to call it that, is it doesn't linger very long or travel far from its source," Harah said. "Before the power outage no other particles were detected, so I'd say you're safe to depart if you aren't feeling symptomatic of radiation poisoning."

"Isn't one of those symptoms puking doc?" Oskar said as he clapped Steppan on the back. "You might want to keep him under observation for a while, purely for safety reasons." Steppan glared at him, then he hit the button to open the exit door.

Divana glanced between the departing detectives and the apathetic doctor, trying to decide what to do. "I think I'll stick around until at least the hazmat team has been through. Is there a place around here where I can use my imbedded mobile? I should probably check in with a few people."

"No, but I can connect you with the building's secure network," said Harah. "You'll be 'Guest9' for the duration of your stay with us."

"I'm honored. Did the first eight guests get as much pampering as I am?"

"Well, all of the deputies who work on this side of the building are considered 'guests' since they rotate details so often, so I would have to say no; they probably don't feel pampered. That does give me an idea though…"

~

Hal Dune sulked in his car at the Broken Yolk Café parking lot for a long while after the standoff with the detectives from the sheriff's office ended. Alleged detectives, Hal corrected himself for the dozenth time.

He sat idle not only because he didn't want to get too far away in case Pris needed his help, but also because he didn't know where to go. The whole mess seemed *way* above his paygrade. Everywhere he stepped had to be checked for landmines and he felt surrounded by them. As much as he hated to admit it, he needed to start from the beginning.

Thinking back, going over all the early data and theories, he landed right back on his first lead; the infinity key. Well, he considered it a lead without having any real evidence. Where did he leave off with that? Hal wracked his brain with the details of the last two days, astonished it wasn't a longer timeframe.

With a start he recalled Pris intending to reach out to Fitzroy's widow. He wasn't sure if she made the time for that but she did send him her contact information. Before he considered what he would say to her the phone was already ringing. An intense-looking woman with eyes red from crying answered meekly. Hal could tell she was barely keeping it together and didn't want anyone to know.

"Hello Mrs. Fitzroy. My name is Doctor Harold Dune. I'm with Defense Intelligence. I'm very sorry for your loss." She stared at him for what felt like a long time before responding. Hal guessed she was either expecting him to say something else or formulating a delicate way to respond without crying.

"You know," she said in almost a whisper, "I've gotten so many calls from the Agency I've lost count and you're the first person to actually acknowledge that this is a loss for me as well. Thank you."

"I never worked with Bredon, though someone I served with in the war speaks very highly of him. Perhaps you remember her; Divana Pris?"

Isabeau Fitzroy's composure cracked ever so slightly and she turned it into a smile. "She's not a person you forget easily. I've tried to picture her as a Marine and imagined someone with enough energy for an entire platoon. You were a Marine as well I take it?"

"Navy Corpsman," Hal said shaking his head. "She was actually a fairly quiet person when I was assigned to the same unit, if you can believe that. Taking it all in, she would say. She also volunteered for every additional assignment that came her way and never complained if they didn't go as planned, but you could tell it still bothered her. She ended up as a bit of a perfectionist, though it was hard-earned."

"That's her to a T Dr. Dune," she said. "What can I do for you?"

"Did Pris happen to call you? Provide any details about your husband's death?"

"She contacted me about fifteen minutes ago. Told me what she could, which was discouragingly very little, yet said it was all there was to go on at the moment. Said either her or a handsome doctor would follow up when they got the chance."

Hal blushed. He was certain Pris said that to get that exact reaction. "Nice to know she can still embarrass me even when she's not around. I'm sorry to say I don't have any new information for you. Did she by chance ask you to check out his office, see if anything was out of place?"

"Yes, she did. I was getting ready to go do that now when I realized I'd never been to his place of work. Thankfully you called before I became a total, blubbering mess."

"You look to be holding it together very well," said Hal. "We're trying to trace his recent movements because him being in San Diego is somewhat of a mystery to us. Was there something he always traveled with? Something he thought was important yet may seem inconsequential to everyone else?" Hal knew he was aiming a little too close to the mark if anyone was listening in, but he didn't want to keep the poor woman on the phone any longer than he needed to.

"Um, well… hmm. I'll have to think about that. Bredon was tenacious about keeping his work and personal life as separate as possible. We converted one of our kid's rooms to an office when they moved out and all he used it for was gaming, with the occasional conference call. Can I connect with you again after I return from his office?"

"Of course," he said. "Me or Pris. If you notice something out of the ordinary don't tell us what it is, just say 'there's something you should see' or what have you. I'm sorry to ask you this, but have you been contacted about your husband's remains?"

That did it. The subject she could no longer hold back tears from. The water works came and didn't stop.

"I'm sorry," she said in a croak. "No. Nobody has told me anything about that."

"You have nothing to apologize for Mrs. Fitzroy. I was hoping someone would've said… something by now. Since the opposite seems to be true, I'll book you a transport to come out here later today, or tomorrow if you prefer."

She thanked him and quickly ended the call before the sobs overtook her. Hal sat unmoving a while longer thinking what else he could have asked her and concluded between him and Pris their bases would be covered.

As if by serendipity, once the thought of her entered his mind, she called to fill him in on the setback at the morgue. She reported no ill-effects and was staying to see what they could find out from the other body.

With no other direction in mind, Hal said he was going to see a friend; a secret squirrel friend in Palmdale.

Chapter Nine: Ex Astris, Scientia

Divana Pris returned to the morgue to find Doctor Harah Ibanez chatting with someone new over an unfamiliar machine. Through the small window into the operating theater she spotted three people buzzing around in yellow hazmat suits, waving what Divana assumed was radiation scanning devices around. Harah turned and they exchanged nods.

"They already cleared this room. Should be almost done in there," Harah said. "This is Cenneth. He's helping me with a theory of mine."

"Welcome to the party Cenneth," Divana greeted. The twenty-something guy didn't turn from his display or even acknowledge his name had been spoken, twice. He had a slight face, so Divana figured he was thin, but wasn't sure because of the thick parka he wore, as if the morgue was an Antarctic expedition. Dr. Ibanez noticed the lack of situational awareness with him as well and merely smirked.

"Getting you signed up to our network gave me the idea that there could be a transmission going to or from that cybernetic eye. If true, I hoped we could hack into it and glean something useful."

"A brilliant plan, for an ME," Divana said with a wry grin. "What's with the crash cart?" That comment got Cenneth's attention. He stopped what he was doing in a jerk and robotically turned his head toward Divana.

"Why do people keep calling it that? Should I know what that means?"

"It's a reference to portable emergency medical equipment that gets packed onto a cart and goes where needed. You're probably not familiar with them because the average hospital rooms have had most of that equipment in your lifetime."

That seemed to appease Cenneth, judging by the shrug and return to his display. The exchange didn't answer Divana's question though. "So, why do we need the jalopy?" Another confused look from Cenneth.

"Given the… extreme response from the other eye by a simple scan, we wanted to take some precautions," Harah said. "Since we're likely to encounter a robust security system, Cenneth here thought it best to isolate the signal in this 'jalopy' rather than our network, just in case."

"Ah, good call. Anything yet?"

"We're utilizing a lot of safeguards, so it's slow going. We're still optimistic…"

"Got something," interrupted Cenneth as if nobody else were talking right then. "I haven't been able to dig deep enough for anything conclusive yet, but this line of code can only be DOD; more specifically their aerospace component."

The two women exchanged glances; Divana took the lead. "How can you tell? The 'aerospace component' I mean."

Cenneth highlighted groups of numbers and continued what Divana now considered his verbal, internal monologue since he didn't make eye contact with people he talked to.

"This first set is spatial coordinates; updating consistent to a standard orbit. The second set is uplink codes for a satellite belonging to the National Reconnaissance Office."

Divana stood paralyzed for a moment processing that information. The matter-of-fact way Cenneth explained it made her mistrust what he said. "How can you be sure of that?"

Without turning around once more, he switched his display to show the Department of Defense seal next to a large warning in a graphic style that looked to be a century old. "I see" was the only reaction she could muster.

Damn, she thought. While she was on the right track with the NRO, this meant that Hal, at least in part, was right with one of his theories. Hopefully he can squeeze some more facts from those squirrels of his. Either way he was never going to let her live this down.

~

Hal approached the city of Palmdale with both excitement and trepidation. He'd wanted to see Lockheed Martin's Advanced Development Programs since he was very young, and possibly even in the womb if his mother wasn't joking when she told him that.

Nicknamed Skunk Works in 1939 after a popular comic strip's mysterious company that made "Skonk Oil", Lockheed's most secretive work took place under that title, though they weren't making faux oil. Being there nearly a century and a half, the ADP has since expanded to other locations throughout North America. Regardless, Skunk Works has remained chiefly in Palmdale and Fort Worth, Texas.

As he pulled into the visitor parking lot Hal wondered why it took him so long to come here. He'd loved aircraft all his life, particularly those that were first of their kind. He could probably name at least a dozen excuses off the top of his head that would've brought him here over the past decade as a Defense Intelligence Investigator, not counting the perfectly legitimate reason he was here now. He made a mental note to return with Sean as soon as possible.

Hal slowly made his way past all the scale models of ages past toward the main entrance: P-38 Lightening, SR-71 Blackbird, EQ-97 Wraith... He felt as giddy as a schoolboy and had to actively force himself to put his game face on before talking to some of the best engineers in the world. He resisted going to the museum entrance, for now, and put self-imposed blinders on toward the less inviting visitor doors right next to the employee entrance.

He stepped into a completely white room with harsh, indirect lighting. There were no decorations of any kind, not even inspirational posters with clichéd slogans on them you often see in waiting rooms. Out of habit Hal looked for cameras and listening devices and found none, yet knew they were there. The only frame of reference in the room was the door he entered from and the only sound was his steadily increasing heartbeat.

"Can I help you?" came a voice from seemingly everywhere. It was soft and patient but Hal couldn't decipher the gender of its owner, assuming it was a real person in the first place.

"Doctor Harold Dune. I have an appointment with Elwin Koehl. I'm a little early." Silence for several moments, until the soft voice returned, making him jump once more.

"Please stand by for an ident chip scan." A hidden panel on the wall slid open to reveal a modern palm reader below what appeared to be a century old cathode ray tube monitor. Hal placed his hand on the reader and the monitor came to life showing his all too familiar statistics in the slightly distorted way those monitors were known for.

"What's with the monitor?" Hal asked the disembodied voice. "I thought the museum was next door."

"Some of our more... experienced associates have a taste for retro technology now and again," the voice said. "There's a lot of history in this building, dating back to long before that CRT. You may enter the door to your right. Dr. Koehl will greet you past the security checkpoint. Thank you."

Hal yanked his hand back while the palm reader panel closed and a hidden door opened to his right. He was chagrined in having missed the seams where the door stood open, mocking him. He also did a double-take thinking the room now looked bigger with the two doors and considered the possibility that was some sophisticated optical illusion going on with mirrors and lighting.

He stepped through a short, multicolored tunnel and exited into the much more familiar office setting facing a man who was a little shorter than himself, with messy dark hair and tired brown eyes. The man's smile however was so bright and electric it seemed to have its own energy supply.

Elwin Koehl was a source of endless passion for his work, and indisputable integrity. Hal met Elwin while he was working undercover with the NCIS. A series of leaked data containing schematics of top-secret submarine equipment was traced to a contractor's shop Elwin ran and Hal was sent in to investigate before the full force of the agency turned the place inside-out.

Hal had the list of suspects narrowed down to three people when the agent in charge wanted to move toward an arrest. When Elwin was informed he was on that list he ordered everyone into work, civilian and active Navy personnel alike, and had them all provide full access to their computers, starting with his own. The guilty party, discovered by lunchtime, turned out to be a second-class petty officer who felt he wasn't earning enough money.

A few of Elwin's top engineers resigned over the incident, claiming he didn't do enough to protect their privacy. Regardless, the case was wrapped up quickly and quietly. The most astounding part to Hal was when Elwin thanked him for his thoroughness, after it was revealed Hal wasn't actually a chief petty officer working there under an assumed name. Shaking his hand now, being charmed by his electric smile, made it seem like they were old friends.

"Welcome to Skunk Works Jerry... or whatever your real name is" Elwin said.

"Hal. Hal Dune. Nice to see you again Doctor Koehl."

"Likewise. I assume that's short for Harold? I guess Gerald wasn't too difficult to remember for that month you were with us."

"Actually, it was one of the more strenuous mission preparations I did. I had to be conditioned to answer to Gerald, then Jerry, all while learning your computer system and projects well enough to pinpoint where the leak came from. Once I got there though I liked the work environment so much I began to drag my feet a little. I was disappointed when my boss at the time wanted to pull the trigger after a few weeks. It was a constant battle to squeeze whatever more time I could manage."

"I'll take that as a compliment! I was very proud of the team I had assembled there. It was difficult to leave them when I did, but I managed to convince one of my engineers who felt slighted to take over for me, maintaining that cohesion we'd built up.

Anyway, you didn't come here to talk about that I'm sure. What brings you here today Jer.. I beg pardon, Hal?"

"I came to ask about defense satellites. What might we have up there and what would someone need to take control of one?"

They made their way to a small interview room where four people could comfortably conference with each other or virtually via a condensed computer suite. Elwin slowly eased into the chair opposite Hal as if preparing to spring out of it at the first sign of discomfort.

"That's a tall order," Elwin said after a moment of contemplation. "It'll come up at some point anyway so I'll just ask now; why do you want this information? The more specific you can be the easier it will be for me when I have to rationalize helping in any small way I can almost immediately after you leave."

Hal explained his theory to Elwin, leaving out specific names and places to avoid denying them later. Once he'd finished laying it all out, or most of it anyway, he decided to revisit his first question while the other man requested some tea be brought to their room.

"That's why I'm thinking this group is trying to either take control of DOD satellites connected to our nuclear arsenal, or some other defensive orbital platform I don't know about."

"Ah, so this is in relation to a criminal investigation or conspiracy? Do I have that right?"

"Yes," said Hal a little too quickly. "Only the beginning of one though. We know something is going on, just not the who, what, or why."

"I see. In that case, I think I can help you, probably not to the degree you're hoping for however. This place, and Lockheed Martin in general, isn't in the business of secret keeping. We make things for the military; not exclusively but predominantly you understand, and those projects have varying levels of confidentiality. I happen to be fortunate enough to be attached to some of the more… experimental projects. You don't seem to be asking about any of that so I see no breach of protocol."

"I appreciate any help you can give me, within bounds of course." Hal was suddenly struck by the feeling someone had already been there asking similar questions not long ago. He made a note to inquire about the possibility.

"There's slightly under ten thousand objects in orbit at the moment. I've been told that at one point, in decades past, that number was almost double that, until efforts were made to 'clean up the sky' as it was called at the time. Most people don't know how it was actually done."

Hal shrugged his shoulders as he sipped his tea. "I figured it was a return of regular spacewalks, or a coordinated effort between the multiple space station crews."

"And you would be right," said Elwin, "at least in part. Those ventures managed a bit over a third of the cleanup effort. The rest was handled by ODIN."

Hal waited for an elaboration only none came. "Odin? Thor's dad decided to steal some thunder for a while?"

"A nice pun but sadly no. ODIN is the Orbital Defense and Intelligence Network. It's a collective of satellites that have multiple functions, one of which is to seek and destroy other satellites."

"What? How have I never heard of this before?"

"You probably have, just under another name," Elwin said with a shrewd panache. "Officially, it was called the Strategic Defense Initiative. The average person knows it by its nickname: Star Wars."

"I remember reading about that, yes. If memory serves, that program only lasted a decade give or take, about a century ago."

"Your memory serves you well. The organization formed around SDI ran from 1984 to 1993, but the research and development spawned from it continued behind the scenes. There was a funding bump forty-some years later and it eventually became the Space Development Agency, managed by the then unseasoned Space Force."

The realization hit Hal like a punch to the gut. Space Force, which was an offshoot to the Air Force in its early days, was connected to every piece of this puzzle! Whomever he'd been chasing was trying to gain control of Space Force assets. Hal didn't think anybody within that fifth branch of the Defense Department was behind it, since their budget was massive and they usually got what they wanted, then again he wasn't counting them out either. Something was still niggling at him as well.

"Why do I get the sense this information isn't common knowledge with you?" Hal asked. "That something, or someone, has sparked this very topic recently?"

Elwin sighed and offered a sad smile. "Funny you should ask that. Word got around here about a week ago that one of the lead managers responsible for creating ODIN had died; murdered actually. She was of course long retired; moved to San Francisco to be near her grandchildren. Regardless, she worked with some colleagues here at some point in her career and we were talking about her contributions after the news broke. Name's Ania Mishima. I never met her, as far as I know, but by all accounts she was quite brilliant and lovely to work with."

Hal was taken aback by that word. Brilliant wasn't a term really smart people used unless they were genuinely impressed, or being facetious, in his experience anyway.

"The loss of greatness affects us all," said Hal. "How did the source of this news find out she was murdered?"

"Didn't ask I'm sorry to say. Didn't expect that information to be relevant to any conversation I might have. Would you like me to inquire? Find out who knew her here?"

"No, no. I'll look into it myself. About my other question; do you know what it would take to control ODIN, hypothetically speaking?"

"Not my area of expertise mate. Probably just a simple matter of getting on the proper system, which likely requires some special equipment to fool it into thinking you're on an authorized server. Nevertheless, I am confident in saying that there will be multiple layers of security; for example, the offensive satellites will be more restrictive than, say, the ones for reconnaissance."

Hal considered that account for a moment before hitting a roadblock. "Ok, how does that help me exactly?"

"Well, if someone really is trying to hijack ODIN for nefarious purposes then the layers can at least slow them down before they can do any real damage. Plus, if something strange starts happening with the lower-level satellites that will be a good indication they've been compromised."

Hal reconsidered his prospects while nodding involuntarily. He tried to figure out who he could contact that actively works with satellites, or space in general, when something Elwin said struck him.

"Which level of ODIN can attack other satellites? How does that work without cluttering up the sky with even more useless junk?"

"Good question, I hadn't considered that," said Elwin. "From what my colleagues said, apparently all levels of ODIN can attack other satellites, only with different means. The spy satellites are capable of connecting with and re-tasking others, depending on their encryption, sending them off to wherever. That, I'm told, is what happened to a lot of what was up there. Instead of building new satellites for our fledgling colonies why not send redundant yet still functional ones from here?"

"Interesting," mused Hal. "I'm guessing the others aren't so neat and tidy?"

"In the sense that technology isn't wasted or destroyed, yes, except I'd argue that developing weapons specifically to knock satellites out of orbit or demolish them in a way that created as little debris as possible is pretty neat, and mostly tidy. Plus, I do believe the hacking feature I described a moment ago is available within all three levels of ODIN."

"I see. Well, the saying 'ignorance is bliss' seems an appropriate response to how I felt before learning about ODIN. I appreciate your candor nonetheless. I'm going to look into the alleged murder of…" Hal checked his notes. It had felt so long ago her name had been mentioned. In reality, less than a few minutes had passed. "Ania Mishima. I know some people in San Francisco who might be able to help out. Would your colleagues who knew her like to know whatever resolution I might find?"

"That's very considerate of you. I will inquire to see how they would like to proceed and get back to you. Unfortunately, I won't be providing you their names without their express permission. That I'm afraid is crossing a line at this venture."

"Understood," Hal said. "I didn't intend for this to be a strictly business call, there's just a lot more moving parts I need to nail down than anticipated. I hope to come back for the full tour."

"It would be my pleasure Jerry… Damn, I did it again!"

Chapter Ten: Acta Non Verba

This is Special Agent Pris. Receiving you Lima Charlie sir," Divana said using military alpha-phonetic code for loud and clear. Deputy Director Wray Corvo filled up her display for the second time that week, this time in her personal office instead of the conference room. His expressionless face revealed nothing of what he was about to say, as usual, but she mentally prepared for the worst, also as usual when talking to him directly.

"Pris. How's everybody holding up over there?"

"Well sir, yesterday wasn't exactly an average day. I told my people to take some time off if they needed it. A few have. Most came in today hoping we have some answers for them."

"I don't doubt it," he said without emotion. "And do we have anything to tell them?"

"Yes and no, sir. We've identified who they worked for; their names or why they were here remain a mystery. I have some educated guesses of the why. That's the score at the moment."

"I see," said Wray. "Do I even want to know where they came from?"

"Probably not. Maybe it'll make more sense to you than me though. They were ultimately from the Defense Department; specifically, the National Reconnaissance Organization."

Wray looked up and to his right; a telltale sign he was thinking hard about something. "Can't say I have any feedback that would be helpful to you. I'll kick over some rocks, see what goes scurrying. What do you think they were looking for?"

"I can't take credit for this theory mind you, but it's been suggested that, if connected to Fitzroy's death, they were looking for what's known as an infinity key."

For the first time since she'd known him, Divana witnessed the NCIS Deputy Director show some emotion on his face, and it terrified her. It was very brief, but for a moment his eyes widened and complexion paled. He composed himself and somehow became more serious than normal.

"Listen carefully Pris. If this is some kind of windup or ruse, I'll be *very* disappointed. It's a shame those weren't better tracked after the war, because in the wrong hands one of those keys can cripple entire countries. I wouldn't trust my own mother with one of them, and she's a saint."

"It's a serious point of inquiry sir," Divana said. "We know Fitzroy's tormentor was looking for something, and his service record puts him in the right place and time to come in direct contact with multiple infinity keys. Entirely possible those are unrelated coincidences, and yes, I know how you feel about coincidence."

"Okay..." Wray paused mid-sentence, uncharacteristically hesitant with himself. "I don't like this at all. I'll have to poke the bear at DOD a little harder than expected. Who else knows about this?"

"Just us and the DIA Agent I've been working with. He's the one who proposed the notion of an infinity key in the first place; I'd never heard of one before then."

"Defense Intelligence? Seems a bit convenient. Can we trust him?"

"He was one of my corpsmen during the war," said Divana. We've saved each other's lives on multiple occasions. He was next to me when ATF Agent Frank Toolin was killed."

"So your incorporation into all this very well could be your connection to either this guy or Fitzroy, or quite possibly both. Do I have that about right?"

"That would not be out of the realm of possibility, sir."

Wray nodded knowingly but didn't pursue the matter. "Okay, don't bring anybody else in on this unless you have to, and then only peripherally. I want this infinity key business either confirmed or ruled out as soon as humanly possible. If it's the former, I want you to destroy it on sight."

"Copy that sir. How will I know if I come across one?"

"They look like your standard flash drives of the time, except for a unique handle and no markings of any kind, save one. By unique I mean it will stand out as somewhat garish, and there will be a Roman numeral etched onto it somewhere."

"I'd ask how you know all this but I'm confident you'll avoid the question. I'll settle for learning how many of these things were made?"

"Don't have a definitive answer for you Pris. I want to say five, but that may just be the number recovered and destroyed. Couldn't even say they were sequential. Either way, I do know each one had a specific purpose."

"I thought they were for breaking satellite encryption?" Divana said with some alarm.

"Well, yes, that's basically true. There are multiple encryptions to protect the different functions though. Communications, command controls, defensive actions… they're generally separate roles with alternate accesses that could be changed at a moment's notice. The trick was to attack more than one area of their satellite network at a time while the infinity key anticipated and relayed any new encryptions."

"Ah, so the keys are simply advanced hacking AI? Simple in concept and not design I mean."

"You could say that" Wray said. "Although if it were to ever gain self-awareness it would make Skynet seem like Johnny Five."

"I have no idea what either of those things are, sir."

"Oh, well, it would be scary. That's what I was getting at. Anyway, you have my direct line; use it when you come to one conclusion or the other."

They disconnected and Divana let out a frustrated sigh she'd been holding in for at least half their conversation. When Hal brought up the possibility of an infinity key being involved, let alone existing, she dismissed it as science fiction. Now she desperately hoped he was wrong.

A buzz from her mobile startled her away from the slew of dark thoughts that had crept in. She didn't recognize the number right away, but when paired with the name she made an audible gasp.

"Mrs. Fitzroy! How are you holding up? Will you be heading my way soon?"

"Divana my dear. I'm doing as well as can be expected I suppose, and it's still ok to call me Iz. As for your other question, I'm actually at the airport now. The doctor you described contacted me to…"

"Wait! I'm sorry to interrupt. We'll discuss everything face-to-face. I don't want to take any chances, even on my secure line. Send me your itinerary and I'll meet you at the airport, me personally. I won't be sending someone in my place, so if you're asked don't fall for it."

"I understand," said Isabeau. "Be there in a few short hours."

They switched off and she immediately rang someone else. He picked up before the music she chose while trying to connect finished its tune.

"You done playing with your secret squirrels, Dune? We need another sit down."

"Ok," he said, "except can I choose the location this time? I'm in need of a good cup of coffee."

~

The Havana 1920 was a Cuban restaurant in San Diego's Gaslamp Quarter, where the most enticing thing on the menu to Hal was their Cubano Cortado.

"You're not getting anything?" Hal asked, immediately tuning out any answers from Pris as the liquid fuel began attacking every corner of his body with a warm energy. Divana let him savor the drink before responding.

"This has to be short and sweet. I'm meeting Mrs. Fitzroy at the airport in a little over an hour and would like some backup."

"Backup? You think she's being followed?"

"I don't know what to think," Divana said. "I just want to be prepared for the possibility. You in or out?"

"Sure, I can cover you. Why couldn't you simply message me to meet you there?"

"I'm taking every precaution I can think of. I also wanted to give you this." She slid a small, black pouch across the table. Hal opened it up and inspected its contents with a grimace.

"A radio?"

"It's the same type Secret Service uses. They won't be expecting that, plus these are very tough to unscramble. I want you to keep your distance, only don't let us out of visual contact. Respond with higher than necessary force if I hit the panic button, or send you hand signals. Copy?"

"Roger that. Anybody else on this detail?"

"No," she said firmly. "I'm under strict instructions to involve nobody else. My boss is evidently well-acquainted with infinity keys and wants me to immediately destroy it if one is indeed in play."

"I see," was the only response Hal could muster. "Does your boss know you're about to meet Fitzroy's widow who may know where it is?"

"If he does he didn't learn it from me. I'm gonna head over. I've paid for this and a second cup of… whatever that stuff is, then I'd like you to take up position somewhere nearby. Keep your eyes open and use your radio to steer us away from potential threats. A tough job at *any* airport, so imagine it's Sean we're protecting and use your best judgment."

She left the café without waiting for a rebuttal. Hal didn't like interposing Sean onto a woman he never met but understood the reason why she wanted him to. He finished his cortado and got the second one to-go; he didn't want to be late and feel the wrath of Divana Pris.

~

The San Diego Airport had gone through many renovations since it was built in 1928, yet it was still relatively small compared to the two larger ones in the state. Despite its size however, it was much quicker to adapt to the changes brought on by vertical take-off and landing aircraft in part due to the airport's single runway.

That advancement for commercial use didn't change the layout of the terminals much though, so Hal found himself scanning the familiar shops and restaurants for anybody who was giving Pris an excessive amount of attention. You couldn't solely watch for people who seemed out of place, he kept reminding himself. That could mean almost anyone.

Hal also tried to avoid the trap of profiling people who stereotypically looked like someone trained in surveillance, which often translated to police or military. That wasn't always true either. The basic idea of surveillance work was where to be during a period of time, and what to do when something happens with your target, which in most cases was to send a simple message. All of that could be controlled by access to well-placed cameras or microphones, which Hal hoped wasn't the case in this situation, so people watching was his only recourse.

Considering all those factors, he marked a twenty-something Asian girl with a partially-shaved head glancing in Pris's direction often enough for him to take notice. There may have been an innocent explanation for the kid's attention, but Hal didn't want to take that chance. He circled around behind and pretended to look over the menu at Phil's BBQ while still observing everyone in his line of vision.

Hal didn't have to pretend for very long. Passengers began to emerge from the designated gate. Pris stood up to make herself more noticeable and the girl became visibly more animated; frantically adjusting her earpiece and starting to record video on her smart glasses. As discreetly as he could, Hal extracted his SVR-10 sidearm and fired a stun bolt between her shoulder blades. She slumped onto the table as if she were unexpectedly struck with the urge to nap, which isn't a too uncommon sight at an airport. Lookout or not, the twenty-something was out of commission for a good fifteen minutes.

Hal quickly holstered his sidearm and scanned the area for onlookers. Stun bolts were quieter and sounded different than other projectiles the selective variable repeater model ten could fire, though it certainly wasn't silent. He concluded that a couple of people might've heard the shot and dismissed it as something else.

Satisfied he was in no immediate danger of being watched or arrested, Hal looked up across the terminal to find Pris ending an embrace with an older yet vibrant woman. They began to walk toward the exit and Hal moved quickly when he heard "on the move" in his ear.

~

I sabeau Fitzroy had followed Divana's request for expediency without question. They wove their way toward the arrivals exit making idle chit chat, but she was too focused on everyone they were passing to fully engage in conversation, and she was pretty sure Iz knew that too.

It wasn't a particularly busy afternoon at the airport, Divana acknowledged. The security exit was in sight now and she began to relax a little, until she saw them.

"Two bruisers hanging around the security checkpoint," Hal said in her earpiece a second later. Bruisers they were. Tall, at least six-foot, four inches with shoulders square enough they could be mistaken for a doorway wearing the right attire. About their clothing, there seemed to be an attempt to dress like they were part of the Transportation Security Agency. With a few seconds of extra scrutiny she could tell they weren't.

"Popping into the lavatory on the right. Make a distraction to draw them away," Divana instructed into the handset clipped to her cuff. She ushered Isabeau into the restroom toward the baby changing station.

"Sorry to be so forthright Mrs... Iz, but can you show me what you brought from your husband's office?" Again, the woman responded without protest, which both relieved and impressed Divana. As Isabeau started rummaging through her bag, Pris looked around at the other bathroom attendees. There was an elderly woman slowly making her way out toward the terminal, a mother with her young daughter, and a petite Indian woman emerging from a stall, heading for the row of sinks.

"This is everything I'd say was personal from his office," said Isabeau. "Despite his long career he never really liked the idea of making himself feel at home while working, so he didn't bring much of himself there in terms of things."

Divana looked over the sparse collection of the man's life: a couple of framed pictures, a shadow box of his naval awards, and a metal thermos mug. She examined the frames of his wedding photo, in his Chief Petty Officer uniform, and the picture of his NCIS graduation for anything resembling a secret compartment. She gave the shadow box the same treatment, though that was much faster since there was nowhere to hide anything. With sinking hopes she grudgingly picked up the thermos.

"You consider this personal?"

"Oh yes," answered Isabeau instantly, surprised by the question. "He's had that thing as long as I've known him. He takes it everywhere he goes. I was surprised to see it on his desk actually."

Divana inspected the thermos more closely now, but didn't see anything out of the ordinary. "This is the same exact one? Not a replacement or duplicate?"

"I'm sure it's the same one; I recognize the dents and scratches. The lid broke a few years ago and I offered to get him a new water bottle. He looked at me like I killed the cat… he loved that damn cat. Said it was one of a kind and he'll get it fixed, after correcting me for the thousandth time to call it a vacuum flask."

Something about that term gave Divana pause. She knew it was an old expression that meant the same thing as a thermos. This particular one looked very expensive, despite its long service. It was of a type no longer made because it created a vacuum in the liquid compartment, as well as the insulated layer.

Instinctively, Divana took the flask to the faucet and filled it partway with water. She secured the lid so it would create the vacuum and gasped when she noticed the bottom plate separate ever so slightly. Twisting and pulling on it did nothing, so the next thing on every Marine's list to try was to bang it on something.

Not wanting one of her husband's sentimental keepsakes to be damaged more than it already was, Isabeau grabbed the bottle from Divana and twisted the lid and baseplate in opposite directions. The bottom slid smoothly open a few centimeters, revealing a hidden compartment.

"You knew how to do that all along?"

"No, but it was the next most logical choice after what you already tried."

Pris regarded her a few seconds before deciding to believe her and resorted to shaking the object out of the flask's base compartment. An object looking exactly the way Wray Corvo described landed delicately onto her palm. Aside from the connector that plugs into a computer, the thing was covered in ornate wood, possibly hand carved, with Medieval-looking symbology. What was definitely etched on it by hand was the IV marking on the bottom.

"The imagery is of Prometheus if I'm not mistaken," said Iz.

"My God," was all Divana managed to say.

"I'll take that, Special Agent Pris. If you please."

The voice was silky yet suggestive, almost hypnotic. Divana turned slowly to see the petite Indian woman holding a gun of a type she recognized but struggled to classify.

"You'll take what, miss…?"

"Don't play coy. That object you just found for me in that drinking container."

"Found for who, exactly?" said Divana. "You're not really going to shoot a federal agent in a public restroom."

"You have five seconds to hand that over, or I'll take it from the bits severed by this augmented pinbeam."

Divana tried very hard not to show her surprise and fear of the weapon pointed at her. The knowing grin that passed over her assailant's face indicated otherwise.

The APB models, referred to as All Parts Burned by her Marine instructors, were laser weapons specifically created for military campaigns against armored targets. The handheld versions were *incredibly* rare since their charge lasted only a few seconds. This was the first Pris had ever seen beyond the occasional image or video clip.

If she were alone, Divana thought, she'd try to either disarm the woman or escape until the charge was exhausted. Mrs. Fitzroy complicated that plan. The look Isabeau was giving implied she would accept any option Pris chose. Still, Divana couldn't bring herself to risk the woman's life without any knowledge of the situation.

"Choke on it," she said while tossing the flash drive to the other woman. At the same moment, Divana pressed the panic button on her handset that sent a repeating alarm to the earpiece for a few seconds.

The Indian woman caught it effortlessly and said, "pleasure doing business with you," as she slowly backed out of the bathroom. The two still standing at the baby changing station breathed a sigh of relief.

"What did you give her that for? We could've taken her," Isabeau said. It looked to Divana she was being completely serious too.

<u>Chapter Eleven: Charade</u>

I'm telling you, it was right here!" Hal's attempt at distracting the two bruisers was reaching its end. He was running out of cards to play.

"And we keep telling *you*, we're not TSA officers!"

"Then why are you dressed like you are, and like each other for that matter? That would be like wearing an orange jumpsuit around the local jail; not a well-thought-out wardrobe decision."

The one to Hal's right inhaled to offer a rejoinder then changed his mind. The other put his hand to his ear and Hal realized they were receiving new orders. At that same moment, a fast-repeating set of tones sounded in his ear. The panic alarm. Without another word to the two big guys, Hal spun on his heel and walked as fast as he could toward the women's restroom, narrowly missing a short, black-haired girl emerging from there.

He pulled his sidearm, poised to run in, when Pris came crashing out, nearly knocking him over. Hal regained his balance and joined the chase.

"Why didn't you stop that woman who came out of the bathroom?"

"Why didn't you say to on the radio?" Hal shot back. "I figured she was fleeing some massacre inside by the hand drier."

"She had us at gunpoint at the time, with a pinbeam… at least that's what she said it was. Looks like she met up with her friends."

The bruiser brothers now flanked the Indian woman and tried to keep up with her fast pace.

"Stop! Police!" Divana yelled above the airport din. The two giants slowed and turned; the woman began to run.

A look of recollection crossed the bruiser's faces upon seeing Hal in pursuit and gleefully reached for their pistols. With Hal and Pris already prepared for that contingency, they picked their targets and fired before the two men could bring their weapons to bear.

The two had somewhat different responses however. The one Pris aimed for dropped to the floor right away, while Hal's seized in jerking motions for a few seconds before tipping over like a felled tree; a somewhat common reaction from a stun bolt.

"Are you using lethal rounds?" Hal asked between increasingly heavy breaths. The exertion of running across the terminal was starting to tire him.

"You can bet *they* are. Any reason why we shouldn't pay them the same courtesy?"

"They're not enemy combatants. We still don't even know who they work for. Besides, you can get more information from people who are still alive."

"In that case, you can stay here to secure your prisoner," said Divana. "Either that or pick up the pace."

Hal got the hint and opted to stay and mollify the gathering onlookers to the downed bruisers, including airport police. Pris went to a full sprint after the woman, not looking the least bit winded, and appeared to be making a call at the same time.

"Hold up there sir, we need to clear this area," one of the police officers said to Hal.

"William Karrde, Army CID," he said. "I'm partly responsible for these two lying on the floor. They're armed and need to be cuffed immediately, particularly the one who isn't bleeding everywhere."

Hal handed over his alias ID, hoping they didn't notice it was the older version. He really needed to update his usable names; Will Karrde was quickly approaching a decade old.

"Ok Agent Karrde, what are we cuffing these men for?"

"Conspiracy to commit murder of two federal agents, bringing weapons into a restricted area under false pretenses, and theft of materiel for the purposes of creating weapons of mass destruction."

The mention of WMDs got their attention and officers proceeded to disarm and detain the bruiser brothers as more men and women in uniform began arriving on the scene. The one Hal had been speaking to, who wore sergeant stripes and no nametag, remained firmly in front of Hal.

"You said you're 'partly responsible' for this situation sir. Who or what are the other parts?" the sergeant asked.

"I am. Special Agent Divana Pris, NCIS. I was in pursuit of the person these two were protecting. She had a car waiting outside and escaped."

The sergeant glanced between the two skeptically while taking notes. "So what joint operation brings Army Criminal Investigation Division and Navy Criminal Investigative Service to this airport?"

"They're here to escort me," Isabeau Fitzroy said from the edge of a crowd of onlookers. "I was carrying something of some importance to national security and they were trying to safeguard it, and me."

"I see," the officer said. "If this thing you had was so important, why didn't you request police escort, or have a bigger entourage than the two of you?"

"Well, for starters, we weren't one hundred percent sure she had the object in question, and she didn't know at all," Divana said nodding toward Isabeau. "Secondly, we didn't want to bring more attention to the situation than necessary, putting our charge further into harm's way."

The sergeant appeared to accept that explanation, begrudgingly. He was about to continue his questioning when he received a message in his earpiece the others couldn't hear. Whatever it was troubled the man, Hal thought.

"I'm told you have a crime scene team outside waiting to be approved entry Agent Pris. What do you intend to do with them?"

"I *intend*, at the very least, to take our prisoner in for questioning. You can accompany, and even participate if you like, but that's my minimum offer. The alternative is a jurisdictional battle that neither of us want. I'm well aware that this airport is city property. I also know it's ran by federal rules and regulations, so jurisdiction is a coin toss at best. What say you sir?

After a prolonged stare-down session he asked "what about the other one?"

"Your call Sarge," Divana said. "I've already been to the morgue today with two more like him; one had something implanted that activated and locked the place down from radiation. Although I'd be happy to pass along the details, that's a Sheriff's Office case."

"Two more corpses? You guys have been busy. Good thing one of you went nonlethal this time, otherwise we'd probably be having a different kind of chat."

Pris had a slight pang of guilt, though she refused to acknowledge Hal's self-satisfied look she could see in her peripheral vision. He was right of course. She would never admit it to him but he was usually right when it came to the law and ethics part of the job.

"Here's my deal," the sergeant began. "Since your scene team is already here and mine isn't they can work their magic. The caveat is my people are going to be present every step of the way. That includes the morgue, and I'll take you up on that offer to sit in on the other's interrogation. This will be our case; you'll just be footing most of the bill. Do we have an accord?"

Divana wasn't sure a sergeant had the authority to make such a deal but shook his hand in agreement anyway. They arranged to meet roughly two hours after her team had finished, and she instructed her lead crime scene tech to extend all courtesies to the airport police. Many of the officers looked excited at the prospect of assisting in the analysis of a fatal shooting, since it was a rarity on airport duty. Her extending the olive branch to the PD notwithstanding, Divana seemed very curt and anxious to Hal during the whole exchange and he wanted to find out why.

"Why don't we get the interrogation started right away? He's probably not going to talk anyway so we might as well start the clock on it."

"Because," Pris said, "I got the plate numbers on the car the woman who stuck us up got away in. Figured it was a government vehicle and started a trace as I requested the scene response team. Got a location hit a minute ago and didn't want them tagging along. You riding with me or separately?"

"Um, I'll ride with you I suppose, and have my car follow on autopilot. Where we headed?"

"A multi-purpose building leased by contractors at Coronado Air Station. I'm sure it's just coincidence that the explosion which started this whole thing is practically a stone's throw away from where we're going."

Hal bowed his head in consensus yet said nothing. He should've considered checking the area for government assets not part of the Navy! Doing a quick search on the way might give them a slight advantage; he hoped it wasn't too little too late to be making these basic assessments.

~

The building wasn't big, two or three stories perhaps, it was hard to tell. Despite its difference in architecture, the place gave Hal flashbacks of a similarly sized building he was trapped in for a few hours in Portland a couple years back. Pris noticed his reluctance and slowed her pace for him to catch up.

"Don't worry," she said. "you're not going in first. There's a tactical team ready to breach on my command."

"You're going to breach? You don't even know which suite they're in! We don't want additional attention on us than we already have with more collateral damage."

"We do know the suite number actually, Mr. Smith. We've already had someone inside to suss out the interior while we were on our way over."

Hal recoiled at being called Mr. Smith. It was an insult derived from the old movie Mr. Smith Goes to Washington. It stemmed from combat veterans being micromanaged by people not anywhere near the action, usually in Washington.

"Well, sounds like you have everything in order then. Let's hope they haven't led us into a trap."

Divana regarded him for a long moment, then gave the order to enter the building.

"Wait, you're not joining them?" Hal asked, astonished she hadn't moved from next to the car.

"I'm the boss now. Bosses aren't supposed to go in with the tactical units. Besides, you're right. Two shooting incidents in two days has me jazzed up a little. You also might be right about the National Recon people; they're the registered owners of the vehicle and have a suite in this building. Before you say anything, I'm giving you a preemptive order to shut up."

Even if she hadn't said it Hal couldn't think of a witty retort due to his disbelief. Instead, he simply smiled and stared until he made her smile back.

After a few minutes, the all clear came through and the two made their way into Building 626. People from the handful of other offices crowded together by their glass doors or ornately decorated waiting rooms, held at bay by NCIS agents in full tactical gear. The National Reconnaissance Office door told a different story.

The same type of placard with suite number adorned the wall like all the others they passed in the building. If that were misread it could be easily confused with a custodial closet. The plain white door was off its hinges, the display on its coded entry, rather than an ID scanner like all the others, flashed ERROR without anyone seeming to care. It was a nondescript corner at the end of a hallway opposite the unisex restrooms.

Following Pris into the suite, however, caused Hal to pause mid-step because he got the feeling of walking into another dimension. Aside from a single open doorway at the end of a short hallway, all available space lining the walls was covered with communication equipment from floor to ceiling.

Every window was blacked out with what appeared to be solar panels, though the room was still well lit by a large LED ring tethered haphazardly to the ceiling. Opposite the light ring, seeming to erupt from the removable tiled floor, was an octagonal table on a single, thick pedestal. The Earth was projected over the table, with thousands of tiny dots hovering around it color-coded into categories Hal couldn't begin to guess what they meant.

Slouching indignantly on the only chair in the room was the woman from the airport. She was putting up a tough façade; arms and legs crossed, scowl adorning her face. Regardless, Hal could tell she was nervous by the way her eyes darted toward anyone who closely inspected her machines.

"She refused to give her name," one of the breach team agents said to Pris. "Palm scan says she's Akeylah Patel, NRO Analyst, out of Leesburg, Virginia."

"We meet again Ms. Patel," Divana said. "You're a long way from Virginia. Came all the way out here to sleep on a cot in the back room of an office made comfortable for machines rather than people? I don't know what deal they sold you on to accept this glorious lifestyle but I promise you, helping us will be a far better one for your sake."

Akeylah Patel's smoldering silence continued. The look in her eyes was a mixture of pleading and rage.

"All righty then, have it your way. Can't say I didn't try. You know why we're here, so where is it?"

Still nothing from their captive.

"Ok, we'll just have to tear this place apart until…"

"If you touch anything this place will explode!" Akeylah screeched loud enough for pilots in the hangars a stones-throw away to hear over the drone of their engines. Pris turned to the team lead for an explanation to the outburst.

"She was disarmed and thoroughly searched. We found no explosive devices ma'am," he said in confident monotone.

"Of course you didn't find them, they're wired into the equipment!" Akeylah said a little more collected than before.

Divana trusted her team but didn't think Patel was bluffing either. "Everyone out. Evacuate the building. Just in case," she added when her team lead began to protest. After a very efficient few minutes, all who remained was Pris, Hal, and Akeylah.

"So now what? You gonna start pulling out my fingernails?"

"No, I'm more of a cut and smash things kind of gal," Divana said. A chill ran down Hal's spine and he stepped forward to intervene. Pris put a hand up to stop him and Akeylah's darting eyes returned in hysteric force.

"Whatever you do to me you're too late to change what's already been done."

"What makes you say that?" Divana asked. Hal was getting a little impatient and started taking a closer look around the room.

"Your drive is over there," Akeylah said, pointing to a particularly busy looking panel near Hal. "It's served its purpose. To regain control of the network however, you'll need a very specific command console, and there isn't one here anymore."

Hal spun around after unplugging the infinity key to regard the two women. "You mean the football for ODIN, don't you? You've made it mobile."

"What the hell is he talking about?" Divana asked Akeylah.

"The Orbital Defense and Intelligence Network," Hal offered. "Not as scary as our nuclear deterrent, not as well protected either I'm guessing."

"I was wondering what he was doing here," Akeylah said. "Your friend is correct. How he came to that conclusion might make for an interesting story."

"You don't have to talk like I'm not here you know."

"So how do we find this football?" Divana said, ignoring Hal.

"I don't want to tell you how to do your job but you can try triangulating the signal to the network."

"Can you do that from here?"

"No. And even if we could there wouldn't be enough time. Once he disconnected that drive a silent timer began. We have maybe two minutes before the place self-destructs."

Her nonchalance gave Divana doubts of the woman's sincerity. She decided to press on despite Hal's imploring stare. "You can't enter in a code to stop it or something? You don't seem very worried about your impending demise."

"There's a minute-long window to enter a code. That red flashing display over there indicates that window has closed. My life was forfeited the moment you busted that door down. You can't ensure my safety from your own government; what's there to be optimistic about?"

Hal checked his watch anxiously and began inching toward the destroyed door. Pris tried to remain calm. "So your choices are to die here in this depressingly stale room, or come with us and maybe die in the near future. What will it take for you to make the latter choice, possibly saving a lot of lives in the process?"

Akeylah considered the offer for an infuriatingly long time, yet in reality it was only a few seconds. "Immunity from prosecution and reassignment off world. I have skills that can be useful anywhere."

"Done. Now let's get moving," Divana said as she took Akeylah's arm in an escort hold. They wove their way through the corridors quickly without running. Their short trek ended with Pris stopping short outside the front doors and looking up at the old military designed building in dire need of remodeling.

"You were bluffing this whole time, weren't you?"

As if in answer, a deafening explosion erupted on the opposite side of the building, followed by several others. Each panel had separate devices and were exploding in series, they later found out, though it was all concentrated inside the one office, not the whole of building 626.

The trio turned and walked directly to Divana's vehicle. Shore Patrol and emergency services were just arriving as they piled in the cruiser, so she barked her last set of orders to the tactical team and sped off before the area was locked down.

"My ears are ringing," Hal said loudly.

"What?" The two women responded in unison.

"Never mind."

"What!?"

Chapter Twelve: Directive 4

The ride back to NCIS was brief and uneventful. Hal spotted his car in the visitor lot outside of Coronado Airbase and instructed it to proceed to the main naval base where he would have to drive it inside; unmanned vehicles were prohibited to enter government installations.

Approaching her building, Divana sank in her seat a little when she saw the San Diego Police cruiser. Although it hadn't even been two hours since they had left the airport, she had forgotten about inviting the sergeant to interrogate the guy Hal had stunned with a taser bolt. She was slightly relieved to learn it had hardly been a few minutes since the officers arrived. Still, she felt unprepared.

Their conference room had become a sort of command center, with the crime scene technicians coordinating with SD PD airport officers as well as the county's crime lab to get immediate results. Divana proudly watched everyone work so diligently until people started to notice her standing in the doorway with a strange grin on her face. She had Akeylah sit in a quiet corner and directed one of her agents to keep an eye on her while she got up to speed.

There wasn't much new to report, she quickly found out. Their captive wasn't talking, not a single word, and he had nothing in the way of identification. The recovered guns were of the same machine pistol type as the pair from the day before, however the serial numbers actually had a hit on the records check. They were listed as being part of a bulk sale of seized property to a "Government Entity." It wasn't much to go on but better than nothing.

"Busy day," came the voice of Sergeant Yeoman of the airport police. He had changed into a more formal uniform than the cargo pants and short-sleeved duty shirt he had on before, and his name was prominently displayed on a gleaming metal tag.

"Very. Been waiting long?" she asked, trying to make small talk while checking the latest report from Coronado.

"Only about ten minutes, probably not even that. Been pretty smooth so far; I thought it would take longer to link up our evidence techs. I overheard you're also coordinating with the county over a shooting yesterday as well. Is that the other trip to the morgue you were talking about?"

Divana grimaced and nodded. "In this very room, barely more than 24 hours ago. Same type of G-men as the airport. Same model of sidearms too if you can believe that."

"Those pocket Uzis? Serious hardware. Not very practical though. Lose anybody from the shooting?"

"No, thankfully," Divana said. "One of them got a few rounds off; clipped a shore patrol officer. I took them both out before they could do worse."

Yeoman looked at her with admiration. "Nice work. What did they want?"

The question hit her like a smack to the face. Hal had taken the infinity key from Coronado, and she dropped him off at the main gate so he could get his car. It shouldn't have taken him this long to make his way back there. Pris gave Yeoman a noncommittal answer and excused herself to track him down.

A number of scenarios flashed through her mind, none of them good. What scared her the most however is she had no idea what his intentions were with the key. He never said what he wanted to do if he ever found one, even sarcastically, which was a rarity for him and added to her concern.

After a cursory search of the premises Divana couldn't locate him, so she called his secure line. There was no answer. She began to shake with unease as she tried his private line. He picked up on the first ring.

"Where the hell are you? I thought you were just picking up your car!"

"I'm fine, thanks for asking," Hal retorted, his demeanor calm to her near hysteria. "I couldn't have been more than a few minutes behind you. Got to the conference room, saw that it was busy, and that sergeant from the airport hitting on you, so I decided to go back to the peace and quiet of my vehicle and get some work done. I do have a job of my own you know."

Divana flushed with shame. She didn't know which of those points to address first. "He wasn't hitting on me."

"Maybe not, but he definitely fancies you. Why else do you think he put on his Sunday best to conduct some interviews?"

She didn't know how to respond to that, so decided to change the subject. "Did you come up with anything useful from your fortress of solitude?"

"Yes and no," he said. "I called my contact at NORAD and asked him if anything unusual was happening with ODIN. He of course couldn't confirm what ODIN is, or that it exists, but claimed nothing out of the ordinary was happening in orbit at the moment. I told him to keep an eye on it and let me know when that changes."

Pris disconnected the phone call when she reached his car and sat in the passenger seat, after he cleared off his jacket and tablet that is. "Ok, so what's the useful part of that?"

"For starters, that tells us they haven't made their move yet, assuming of course that was their intention all along. We also have more people checking the eyes in the sky. With any luck, somebody's testing the command access codes right now to see if they still work."

Divana acquiesced and let out a breath she didn't know she was holding. It was relieving that the group of dissenters hadn't taken any more action yet, though still concerning she didn't know where the people they're chasing are or what they planned to do. She would have to talk to Akeylah again, and prioritize the interrogation. Before that, there was another matter she had to conclude first.

"Can I have the infinity key, please?"

"What do you plan to do with it?"

"I plan to destroy it, as ordered," she said.

"It's not yours to destroy. I believe it's the property of Mrs. Fitzroy. Have you checked in with her by the way, since you shipped her off to a hotel?"

Divana winced at the question, not wanting to answer it and suspected he only asked to distract her. She wasn't going to play that game.

"Don't change the subject. And you know damn well I don't need permission to neutralize bona fide threats to national security."

"I remember reading that somewhere too," Hal said. "Good thing it already *is* neutralized, by being under our control. Besides, don't you think we should hang onto it a little longer so we can potentially reverse whatever it was just used for… assuming your friend was telling us the truth?"

Damn him! He was right of course, she admitted. "Fine, we'll try it your way, for now. Any bright ideas on how I phrase it to my boss that I disobeyed an order?"

"Yes, don't tell him you have it yet. It's not a lie, even by omission, since I have it. If he asks you directly say what I just told you. Now, I know we need answers quickly so do you want me to talk to that girl from Coronado while you're in interrogation, or keep trying to find someone directly related to ODIN?"

"I'll talk to her," Divana said. "She didn't seem to acknowledge your existence last time anyway. Do you have any more leads to follow up on or just possibles?"

"A bit of both. One of the architects of ODIN was murdered in San Francisco recently. I want to see if there's more to that story. I'll talk to my secret squirrel again too."

She agreed and reluctantly departed his old cruiser, after he assured her that he wasn't going anywhere. Once the door to the building closed behind her Hal let out a sigh of relief. For a moment, maybe even a full minute, he thought Pris was going to pull her weapon on him. It wouldn't have been the first time; during the war she tried to force him to give a squad-mate medicine who was too far gone for it to be of any help. He held out hope she had learned to trust his judgment and thankfully it worked out in his favor, at least this time.

Hal gathered his thoughts and searched his contacts for a San Francisco Police Officer he met over eight years ago, predating his time with Defense Intelligence by only a few days. When he found the name in the directory his finger hovered over the touchscreen hesitantly. The last time they'd spoken was at the funeral for his partner who died before Hal's eyes. After several mental edits he finally worked out what he wanted to say and dialed the number.

"Hello Officer Jon Colquitt, it's Hal Dune. I hope you remember me because that will make this a lot easier."

~

Divana Pris sat across the interview table from the big man Hal tased at the airport. She traded glances with Sergeant Yeoman seated next to her after the only two words their prisoner spoke confused the situation even more than it already was.

"Directive Four doesn't apply to you because we haven't confirmed your identity or employment status yet," she said. "Even if you did decide to properly introduce yourself, this isn't a federal case, that's why the Sergeant here read you your rights and not me or one of my agents. So, while that may not inspire you to start cooperating, I just want to know one thing, then I'll release you into the capable hands of the PD where you'll be able to contact your attorney, or whomever you like."

The man across from her nodded marginally, but it was enough to perceive an answer. The man next to her shifted in his seat uneasily.

"Where were you headed after Coronado? Where is your home base? If these are two different places I'll settle for where everything is supposed to go down. Don't pretend you don't know what I'm talking about."

The bruiser stared unblinkingly for several moments weighing his options. His bionic eye had been damaged from the taser bolts, so he couldn't transmit or self-terminate. His imbedded chip deleted itself when it was scanned by a police data assistant, so he had nothing to barter with. The fastest way to get out of his current predicament was to give them something, verbally. His loyalty was to the highest bidder and right now there was only one offer that mattered.

"Old Top Gun," he eventually said.

The voice was so deep and robotic Divana wasn't sure it came from a human being. He repeated the phrase again then folded his arms, indicating that was as helpful as he was going to be.

"Old Top Gun? What does that even mean?" He had returned to his primary status of a breathing wall so Divana ended the interview in a huff. She walked straight out to where Akeylah sat, looking supremely bored. Yeoman struggled to keep up.

"Where did your bodyguards at the airport come from? Where is the next nearest NRO office?"

Akeylah sat up with annoyed slowness. "I don't know. Why don't you ask them?"

"Him," Divana corrected. "One of them is dead, and I'm beginning to think the other isn't competent enough for normal human speech. Was there a code word or phrase you overheard that might indicate another location nearby?"

"No. I'm not important enough to come across that kind of information, even accidentally. The NRO is almost exclusively set on the east coast. I worked out of a secret location and it was the only one I know of. I was hours away from completing my assignment and leaving that hole forever when you showed up."

"Hours? Is that an accurate estimate or an approximation?"

"After I helped them hack into ODIN all I had left to do was wait for them to test their command of the system," Akeylah said. "I would then receive a message telling me to shut down operations and where to rendezvous. So to answer your question, I guess both."

Divana was beginning to lose her patience. "You say you're not important enough for basic information yet seem to know a lot about the overall plan. Do you know why seizing control of that satellite network is so imperative?"

That question seemed to get Akeylah's attention. "Recognition. A seat at the proverbial table. Upwards of seventy percent of all intelligence comes through satellites. We track and catalog every single one of them; that's the extent of our authority. You think I was lied to about being confined to that office for almost six months? I volunteered once I found the reason why."

"Ok. What do they plan to do with the satellites now that they have control of them? You don't really think everyone is going to just sit back and accept this as anything but a hostile takeover, or possibly even a terrorist attack, do you?"

"There isn't much choice left in the matter. They'll probably have a public spectacle to make their point for all to see, then leave it up to the talking heads to either accept terms or receive another demonstration. Now, when can I expect my off-world transport?"

Divana couldn't help laughing out loud. "You can expect to be *escorted* off-world to the most hole-in-the-wall colony I can find when this crisis is over and you've outlived your usefulness, in that order. And God help you if that 'public spectacle' hurts anybody, directly or indirectly."

"In that case, I invoke Directive Four, since it looks like you're reneging on your agreement with me that I accepted in good faith."

"What is it with you people and Directive Four!" Pris's outburst got everyone's attention in the room. "Whomever told you about that didn't know what they were talking about. It's not a get-out-of-jail-free pass. I will keep my word and not seek prosecution against your bathroom antics. Mine isn't the only agency concerned here though. You're also an important witness who has vital information of a criminal plot that involves treason and blackmail. All of those points invalidate Directive Four, and as far as your transport off-world, you should've specified a timeframe. Van den Berg! Take her to an interview room please. Leave her some food and drink; might be a while until we get back to her."

Akeylah left without protest, however the look on her face felt like it raised the temperature of the room a few degrees. Divana watched her go, wondering if she was wasting her time and thinking darkly if it would've been better served leaving the girl in Coronado. She didn't know how long it had been but she eventually noticed Sergeant Yeoman standing at her elbow.

"Yeah, so I checked out what that blockhead in interview said and it looks like Top Gun is the Navy fighter pilot program in central Nevada. The official name is Strike Fighter Tactics Instructor or Fighter Weapons School."

"Oh, right, thanks. You mean to tell me he was actually giving us a clue as to where the rest of his miscreants were going?"

"Seems that way," Yeoman said. "I can't be sure if that's what he meant by '*Old* Top Gun' though."

"Old Top Gun is in Miramar, not twenty miles north of here," Hal interjected from the doorway. "It moved to Fallon, Nevada sometime in the mid-1990s. Miramar is still a Marine Air Station however, so that might explain their incursions into other Marine bases."

Pris stared at him openmouthed, shocked that a second person had approached her unnoticed. "Thank you for that timely information. Did that just come to you or are you trying to steal Yeoman's thunder?"

"I just received word that ODIN has activated, and not by its operations center in Maryland. They traced the signal to Miramar. I came in to pass that along and stumbled into the topic of Top Gun. Am I the only one around here who watches movies made before my time?"

"You know, you really might be the only one," Divana said with a wry grin. "Kimura! Do we have any assets working in Miramar? We might need them to roll out the carpet for us."

"I think so, I'll confirm that and make contact."

"Thanks. How about you Hal? Anybody there you can call? I don't want to just show up in a convoy of NCIS vehicles without any kind of warning."

"I don't, but Lindsey might. I'll give her a call."

"Ok people, we have a group of government employees who have taken control of a top-secret satellite network. I don't want a hundred questions about details of this situation, mostly because I don't have all the answers and we don't have the time. The only relevant points you need to know right now are these satellites have offensive capability and control of them has been taken away from their liable authority for political or personal gain. I need tactical plans for any fortifiable buildings at Miramar with a high amount of communications gear in twelve minutes. Everyone field certified be ready to fly in fifteen. Get to work!"

Everyone snapped to it, despite only knowing part of the story. The tactical team in Coronado had been recalled to meet them in a staging area outside the base, that's where Hal received the return call from his wife.

"Talked to the executive officer of Miramar; we were at Annapolis together. He was pretty pissed off this was happening under his nose. I had to convince him from shutting the base down and personally kick in every door to find them. He assured me he'd settle for being part of the welcoming committee. He's got thirty-five marines standing by, plus himself and his adjutant. I'll connect you to coordinate." Before disconnecting she added, "come home alive, and show them treason is still our most serious crime."

Chapter Thirteen: High Fidelity

The sun had gone down and the moon had risen by the time everyone was in position. The moon was either full or no more than a couple days away from being full, Hal couldn't tell on sight alone. What he was sure of though is that it had taken far too long to triangulate the uplink signal and clear the surrounding buildings. It was a safe bet their opposition knew they'd been found.

Close to seventy Marines, San Diego Police, and NCIS personnel were stationed around a pair of buildings off Bauer Road connected by an underground passageway. Before the scattering of fortified bunkers were built around the base, armaments and ordinance were kept in underground storage rooms to protect against aerial bombardment and visual espionage. One of these subterranean warehouses eventually became a backup air traffic control center with equally advanced communication equipment. That's where the wayward NRO group decided to dig in.

Early reports from disguised scouts indicated there were armed lookouts on each floor of both buildings, which infuriated the base XO even more because one of the buildings was supposed to be closed for renovation. Everyone was poised to advance on the twin structures when word came through that ODIN had made its public debut.

Video feeds from all over the night side of the Earth showed what appeared to be a meteor shower. Some of the clips Hal came across were strikingly beautiful and he began saving them to his cloud when it was revealed what the falling objects were: satellites. Dozens of them, perhaps hundreds. Their flimsy exterior of antennae and solar panels melted off rapidly, leaving the reinforced batteries or miniature nuclear cores as the final part of their structure to survive entry into the atmosphere.

With everyone's attention firmly on the skies, the demonstration's second act was timed perfectly for the world to witness. The offensive side of ODIN was put into action by defacing the moon. Or, more accurately, made the man on the moon's face more defined. Hal didn't know if that was the intended result or a happy accident. It was the most terrifying yet strangely satisfying thing he had ever seen.

Divana, on the other hand, had seen enough. She was doing her best to get everyone refocused on the raid when a shot rang out, echoing through the surrounding buildings.

"Who fired that shot? Report!" She said on the operational frequency.

"It came from the third floor of the east building, we're under attack. We have a Marine down, need a medevac," came the sobering response. Divana didn't hesitate.

"Copy that. Sniper teams, pick targets on all floors above one and engage. Team alpha, blow all doors and provide covering fire. Team bravo, blitz entry into both structures. Team Charlie, evacuate wounded and keep your head on a swivel for any counterattacks from outside the target area. Go!"

With seemingly rehearsed precision, the buildings erupted in nearly simultaneous gunfire and controlled explosions. Mere seconds had passed as bravo team reached the now gaping doorways amongst a smattering of covering and return fire. It was at this moment Divana asked Hal to go treat the wounded Marine, and any others that may need patching up which, based on the reports in his ear, there were a few. He wasn't sure whether or not to be disappointed to be missing out on the action or relieved to not be amid the wounded. Being the only medic on scene, he was exactly where he needed to be.

The gunfire began to abate, and eventually the staccato shouting that came with room clearing waned and then stopped completely. Four more people were escorted over to Hal with graze and concussive wounds, arriving just in time to see the first injured Marine die from a well-placed shot around his body armor. The others were patched up and alternated with team Charlie for the next phase of the siege.

Access to the underground tunnels was obstructed by thick metal doors. Not as formidable as vault or bunker doors yet heavy enough to grind their egress to a halt. As Divana was about to call for a laser torch one of the Marines had another idea and ran off to a nearby building. He returned moments later with a slender, mean-looking object that he wielded like a medieval weapon, and wasted no time assuring a skeptical group of people that it would be better.

"It's a cutting tool we use to get pilots out of crashed planes whose canopy won't open," the Marine said. "We call it the lightsaber because it'll cut through most anything in seconds; at least half as fast as your average laser torch."

Divana presumed the guy was looking for an excuse to use it but she didn't want to set them back more than they already were. She told him to get to work, and had the breach team ready their flashbangs and low range EMP grenades. The young Marine was right. The lightsaber cut the hinges off faster than alpha team could prepare to enter the underground room with an unknown layout. Due to this they skipped the electromagnetic pulse and tossed in two flashbangs and one x-ray probe once the door was pried open.

Almost instantly, the breach team started receiving 3D telemetry from the probe and had enough intel of the space beyond as well as the level of opposition they were facing to form a plan of attack. Within twenty seconds of the door being sliced open team alpha were scampering in the room barking orders to whomever awaited beyond.

They were yelling into an empty room. The only things staring back at them were the multitude of displays adorning the walls. The x-ray probe was recalled from the ceiling where it floated and the opposite door was opened to the remainder of alpha team.

"Charlie, check for heat signatures in sewer grates and access hatches. Bravo, start clearing surrounding buildings again; pattern at your discretion. They're here somewhere people, just have to find which spider hole they're hiding in," Divana said as she made her way to the underground comms center, collecting Hal along the way.

The room was disturbingly similar to the NRO office in Coronado. So much so that Hal considered it likely one of the two locales was a purposeful recreation, prompting a chill to run down his spine from recalling what happened to the other place.

"Maybe we should EMP this place after all," said Hal. "To deactivate any timers or electronic detonators that could be rigged up in this machinery."

Divana pondered that a moment before responding. "I think that other place was a facsimile of this one, which they didn't build, so it's doubtful they took all this apart to wire it with Semtex. Having said that, the odds have been against us this whole time, so why should they swing our way now? Zim, prepare some EMPs to blanket this room. I want…"

"Agent Pris, this panel is movable. Scans show vacant space behind." Divana didn't recognize the speaker behind all the tactical gear, and finding out didn't cross her mind now that at least one crucial mystery had been solved.

"Right. Ok, let's zap the place first then I need ten volunteers to accompany me inside. Where's that XO? See if we can't get a map of the old tunnel system that's 'supposed' to be sealed off."

~

The whole affair only took a few minutes, though the amount of instructions that were passed during that time was astonishing. Miramar's Executive Officer wasn't comfortable with the idea of shutting down their backup air traffic control, until he learned what happened at Coronado.

Then there was a debate about the existence of underground passages; Divana had to show footage of its entrance as evidence in order to move forward with obtaining any intel on them. Thankfully the old system wasn't vast and only extended to three more buildings, two of which were across Bauer Road.

Bravo team verified the closest connected structure was still clear, and confirmed the tunnel access was sealed up by concrete. Charlie team converged on the remaining two buildings, which were listed as ordinance workshops so they maintained their distance in a perimeter. That left a third of alpha team, along with Divana and Hal, to flush the errant NRO members one direction or another.

They split the team into two groups that hugged each wall. It was dark though not pitch black, so only the lead members of each team used night-vision visors. There were no side rooms or cover of any kind to hide behind. For an underground warehouse that hadn't been used in over a century and was supposed to be sealed off it, was in surprisingly good condition, Hal mused.

When the opposite end of the corridor began to materialize in his unenhanced vision, Hal could just make out what was likely a duplicate of the doors they had cut their way through. The low lighting made shadows play tricks on his eyesight but there seemed to be something in front of their exit obstructing the way. He wasn't sure what it was from the back of his line, yet had the distinct impression he saw tires. His answer came a few seconds later.

"There's a motorized cart situated between the doors," one of the point men said over the comms. "There appears to be a trip wire approximately one meter in front…"

The report was cut off by the cart abruptly being engulfed in flames. Not so much exploding as spontaneously combusting. The two using night-vision snoopers were temporarily blinded and fell back in their respective lines to recover while the next person took point. There didn't seem to be any other injuries, so it was assumed to be a diversionary tactic, until the coughing began.

Like a wave that struck in succession, the sensation of burning eyes and uncontrollable coughing took effect on everyone. Divana knew right away what it was.

"Acid fire! If you have masks put them on. Press forward and take position around the doors. Alpha team, have bravo and Charlie do some luring fire. We breach in 30."

They were simple enough commands however they all had an asterisk next to them. Only about half the tactical team members present had breathing masks, so they had to guide the others who didn't which allowed time for the poisons in the atmosphere to intensify. While luring fire was a good idea if it worked to draw out any of the remaining aggressors it was far from a guarantee. It was the perfect trap.

Then there were the doors themselves. Everyone appeared to be in position, haphazardly, and Hal didn't see anybody moving to set blast charges or prepare a battering ram. In the growing smoke and painful burning in his eyes he could barely see Pris approach each door with a long object and make a fast, decisive motion on them before returning to her place at the end of the group.

The next minute was a total blur as his consciousness began to fade. Hal heard some loud bangs, followed by shouting mixed with gunfire, though he could see only dark shapes and flashes of light. Eventually, the picture began to clear. He could feel his legs moving him toward the light as if they were outside of his control. Once he crossed the threshold into the next building the chokehold that was asphyxiating him began loosening its grip.

Hal blinked the accumulated tears from his eyes and fought the urge to rub them. Looking around the room he could see others in the same predicament; he reminded them not to rub their eyes too. Everything seemed to have an aura around it, which suggested that he was hypoxic since he wasn't prone to migraines. He didn't dwell on that though; he could see others were far worse off than him.

Leaning up against the wall of the basement room was the deceased, alpha team members and people in plain clothes alike. Next to them were the severely wounded who needed triaged, so Hal shook off a little more of his dizziness and stepped in to assist the arriving medics.

Despite her massive headache, Divana was trying to coordinate cleanup efforts to the standoff they had just ended. All hostiles had been neutralized and she was hoping at least one of those still alive knew how to operate the device she held in her hand. A device Hal referred to as the nuclear football, which wasn't much more than a computer built into a briefcase.

The last of the ambulances had arrived, or so Divana was told, and she allowed herself a relieved sigh. The operation could've gone better: two dead agents, six more wounded, along with three injured Marines. It also could've been a lot worse, given the circumstances of poor intelligence and well-prepared adversaries.

That last point raised a question in her mind; did the National Reconnaissance Office really have *that* many resources and military trained personnel at their disposal? Perhaps throughout the entire agency, she mused, however she doubted they were all in on the conspiracy and had all converged in southern California to carry out their plans. No, someone else had to be helping them.

"I want IDs on everybody as soon as possible. Use whatever means you can think of to get it done," she said while heading back into one of the buildings to look for Hal. She passed an EMT moving in the opposite direction in a hurry, nearly knocking her over, and didn't think anything of it until she made it into their designated triage area.

Injured agents and Marines were being treated by a swarm of medical personnel buzzing around them. She expected Hal would be among them, then her peripheral vision drew her attention to his tan mackintosh, along with the rest of him in a heap in the corner. She nudged one of the medics to ask what the problem with him was.

"I think he was complaining of hypoxia after field dressing a couple shrapnel grazes. One of the other guys gave him some oxygen... I don't see him here anymore."

Divana knelt beside Hal and felt his wrist. He had a pulse, steady and rhythmic as if he were sleeping soundly. She lightly smacked him and called his name; all he did was groan and slightly shift positions.

"Do you have something that can wake him up? He's not injured so far as I can tell. I need him alert to explain what happened."

"I can give him some epinephrine. That'll get him going but it looks like all he needs is a little time and he'll be fine."

"If my suspicions are correct, we don't *have* time. I can do it if you're not comfortable administering." The medic injected Hal with an epipen and backed away without another word. Hal stirred a few moments then his eyes shot open like he was struck by a jolt of electricity.

"What the hell! Was that really necessary?"

"You tell me, you're the doctor," she answered. "But before you tell me, show me you still have the infinity key."

Hal began lazily patting his pockets, then sat bolt upright and patted them again in earnest.

"Damn, I *thought* that EMT with the oxygen was getting a little handsy before things went dark. And here I was going to ask him for a drink later."

"Really? You let somebody pick your pocket like a rube and that's all you have to say?"

"This isn't the first time you've seen me on epinephrine. Might as well give me wine and chocolate while we're at it. That isn't all I have to say by the way. I think I recognized the guy."

Chapter Fourteen: Anti-similitude

The San Diego Naval Base reached a capacity of personnel and activity not seen since the war. So many people had descended on the place that the base hospital's secure ward had to be commandeered until everyone injured at Miramar could be processed. Representatives from the Central Intelligence and National Security Agencies were now included in the growing number of organizations at the NCIS Field Office conference room. It was an all-hands-on-deck meeting for everybody involved, except one.

Hal had respectfully declined the meeting to check something out at his office with Defense Intelligence. Pris didn't want him going alone, though she couldn't come up with anyone to accompany him when she asked.

"Relax," he'd said. "They're not going to kill me in my own office, whomever 'they' are at this point."

So there he was, perusing the quiet hallways of his home base at close to midnight. There was always somebody around, since the work of the Agency didn't end with the setting of the sun, but he could neither see nor hear another soul besides the armed security guard at the one and only checkpoint.

Hal walked past his own desk and headed directly to his boss's office. He touched a button on her desk that transitioned the glass walls from transparent to opaque and sat down reluctantly. She had given him her supervisor access codes, so hopefully she didn't have a problem with him using them at her own desk. His reasoning was that if they were flagged for being used it would appear less suspect at her own workstation. He logged onto the Agency's personnel page using Anessa's passcodes and began wading through employees' biographical data, starting with Bredon Fitzroy's department.

It didn't take Hal as long as he thought it would, hardly fifteen minutes, and he was staring at the man posing as a medic at Miramar. A man who was also present at the bombing where agent Toolin died. Hal didn't think he noticed him at the Kettner Exchange rooftop bar, however he was certain the man was amongst those gathered in the parking lot before Hal made a strategic departure.

The images on the large, curved display stared back at him as Hal compared them to those on his flex tablet, sent by Jon Calhoun. The smaller screen images were captured by neighboring home security cameras after a murder in San Francisco, because the system at the scene of the crime was disabled. While it was certainly possible he could be wrong, to Hal's eye the images were of the same man.

Orlan Rebelo had a round head and dark, dead eyes. He looked like a child's drawing of a smiley face, if he was indeed smiling that is. Hal couldn't picture the man with a smile and concluded he lost that capability ages ago, if he ever had it.

Military Asset and Repurposing Section didn't have much in the way of a hierarchy outside of its supervisor, Arkady Mosin. If it were based on field visits to military owned or ran sites, Rebelo would have a commanding lead, with Fitzroy tailing closely behind in a very literal sense.

Unredacted parts of his service record were also available: he worked logistics for the Army Corps of Engineers for most of his career, which followed a brief stint with Army Explosive Ordinance Disposal where he earned a bronze star. Few details were given regarding how he came to earn that medal, though there was a notation stating he refused the award. At first Hal presumed that was due to post-traumatic stress or survivor's guilt, however a quick search of the incident revealed a lack of quality intelligence resulted in two EOD teams being almost entirely wiped out. Unsurprisingly, Rebelo's medical history was not available in his file; at least some things were still secret!

Recruitment into DIA was the usual business as well: a point system based on knowledge, skills, and abilities. Hal was about to move on to the next section of the personnel page when he noticed that Orlan Rebelo was recommended to the Agency by someone he recognized, the late Decland Quinn. Thick as thieves the two were, not working in the same job but often in the same places geographically.

Quinn's file was equally unhelpful. Hal was prepared to return to Rebelo's file when he noticed a notation on the last page saying "Flagged by Limitations Division for Inquiry". The flag was a link that Hal hesitantly selected which brought him to a list of other flagged files, twenty-three in all. Rebelo, as well as others whom Hal was familiar with, was also on that list.

Uploading this list to any of his mobile devices would be recorded on the system's log, so he did the next best thing; slowly scroll through the names while recording with his flex tablet. When he'd finished, Hal switched back to Rebelo's file and skimmed to the last page to make sure the same link as Quinn's was present. It was.

With something finally to go on, Hal presumed it best not to press his luck on Anne's computer. Even the least observant person would eventually notice a mysterious glow coming from the supervisor's office. Hal returned everything to the way it was when he arrived and slipped back out to the dead silent hallways and work spaces.

Proceeding to his own desk to send a few messages before finally going home, Hal couldn't help feeling that something was off. Looking around he didn't notice anything out of place. Nothing was moved or missing, as far as he could tell, and his desk drawers were still filled with useless junk he didn't want to keep at home. No thieves or neat freaks wanting to boost his level of tidiness. So what was it?

"What brings you in at this hour, Dune?"

Alun Longabaugh. Hal should've known he'd be here lurking about when nobody else was around. What Alun did at the Agency was a mystery to Hal, however the man was several years senior to him, and it was an office faux pas to question his contributions.

"Just sending a couple messages on the hotline. Keeping the home fires burning Alun?"

"Somebody's got to hold down the fort," he said. "Say, you haven't seen the boss around, have you? I could've sworn I saw her office light on a few minutes ago."

"Sorry, that might've been me. She's the reason I came in; trying to catch her during one of those strange schedules she keeps. I poked my head in her office and may have activated a motion-sensitive light. Guess I'll have to hotline the news instead."

"No worries partner. What's the big to do?"

"NCIS had a shootout over at Miramar earlier today, something related to that business on the moon I'm told," said Hal. "They think there might be Agency people amongst the dead and wounded so I wanted to give the boss a heads-up."

Alun was quiet for several seconds before responding; a pensive look on his face. "Where are you getting your info from? What I mean is why is it coming to you instead of this office? I haven't heard about *any* of this… except the stuff about the moon of course. I think the whole world's heard about that by now."

Hal searched his memory for something other than a direct connection to Pris. Everyone he regularly socializes with in the office, which admittedly isn't many, would say Longabaugh is aloof, if they were being particularly kind that day, but Hal didn't buy the man knowing nothing about the last couple days.

"Miramar's Executive Officer knows my wife. He must've remembered I was DIA from a party a couple years back. She got him in touch with me while he was coordinating with NCIS."

"Huh, small world," Alun said. "I look forward to reading your brief on the hotline. If you see Kynes, can you let me know? I have to bend her ear on something."

"Will do." Alun drifted away as silently as he had appeared. Waiting until well after he had gone out of sight, Hal checked the list of names from the video he'd taken. He skimmed through the list twice and didn't see Longabaugh's name. While he couldn't say he was surprised, Hal still let out a relieved sigh he didn't know he was holding. That out of the way, Hal logged onto the hotline and entered in a brief report so Alun wouldn't become suspicious.

The hotline was a repository for critical information available to everyone in a law enforcement capacity, except limited in where entries can be made and how much information can be added. Hal had heard that before those restrictions were implemented, the hotline had been a dumping ground for every little piece of information someone in the field believed was important, often without context or in a format that was difficult to verify. To cut back on useless data it was soon deemed that only supervisors could upload in the field, and everyone else could at a physical office with peer review.

Once finished he gathered up his things and slipped out as unobtrusively as possible, not wanting to engage anyone else until he could further investigate the inquiry list.

~

Divana Pris had enough people to question to keep her busy for the next few days. Although some were still in surgery and several more weren't talking, there were still plenty more who she needed statements from and were willing to provide. She rubbed her eyes; they felt like sandpaper. The adrenaline from the shootout had worn off long ago and she realized how tired she was.

Looking around she could tell everyone else needed a battery recharge as well… except maybe Takashi; he looked like he'd just woken up. Perhaps he drank one of those energy drinks he was rumored to have a large supply of, Divana wondered.

The multi-agency meeting had concluded only moments ago and it was purposefully brief; relaying what happened at Miramar, and what progress had been made with the other related cases, if any. Most seemed satisfied with the results, while some were annoyed they weren't invited to the airbase raid. The rest were checking the clock as if it were a Friday afternoon before a holiday weekend.

"Ok people, unless you're on duty or actively working on something urgent wrap up what you're doing and call it a day. We can pick this back up in roughly, seven and a half hours."

There were a few disappointed murmurs about still coming in at the regular time but nobody had the energy to argue the point. They filed out like a herd of dejected cattle.

"What about you, boss?" Van den Berg asked without slowing her pace to the door.

"Right behind you. I'm waiting to hear back from our DIA contact."

At that moment, Hal burst through the exiting crowd. Julie shrugged and continued on her way out.

"There's a list of flagged names within our agency's database. Thought we could compare it with the few names you've managed to get from your arrestees," he said between breaths.

"You could've just sent me the list instead of coming here and we might both be home by now."

"I didn't want to incriminate you in anything if either of us were investigated by sending it, if you know what I mean."

"Fair enough," she said. "Who made the list?" Hal looked at her as if she had just spoken in another language.

"Who put the list together, and why?" she repeated. "For all we know the Agency could be starting a baseball team. I have an idea for a mascot; the DIA Dunes. What do you think?"

"Wow, you really are knackered. Only time your jokes get worse is if you're drinking. Um, no I don't have those answers, but there's an authorization ID at the bottom of the page, I just need to figure out who it belongs to."

Divana grabbed the tablet from him and perused the names. The number was in the ball park of what outside help she presumed NRO would need to pull off their operation. "I see four names off this list that match people in the hospital, and seven more from fingerprint returns of some of the deceased. Five others have been identified as contractors."

"You remember all those names?"

"The active list is projected right behind you."

"Oh," said Hal.

"It's probably safe to assume that the people we have yet to identify have a high enough security clearance to receive an encrypted embedded chip from either one of those organizations."

"Or another agency entirely."

"Do we have any evidence a third group is involved?"

"No," he said. "We still shouldn't count out the possibility."

"This whole thing was done to gain recognition. 'A seat at the table' Akeylah said. The NRO couldn't do it alone so they made a deal with like-minded people in another agency who have access to nearly every military installation in the Defense

Department. A strategic deal, just not one that would need many concessions. Adding a third party would complicate matters too much, forcing them to share in their narcissism."

"Now who's making theories?"

"Fine, I won't discount the possibility of a third party," Divana assented. "Now, what lead you to finding this list of co-conspirators?"

"Oh right, I almost forgot. I recognized the man who drugged me and stole the infinity key. He was at the bar when Frank was killed, and he's suspected of murder in San Francisco; the victim being one of the original architects of ODIN. I had a hunch he was connected to either Fitzroy or Quinn and it turns out he worked with both of them at some point."

Hal showed Pris the images from the San Francisco Police Department. She perused them with a slight look of recollection showing. "If he was a witness at the Exchange, he should be on the police report."

"He is," said Hal taking the flex tablet back and manipulating it to the desired page. "Identified himself as Orlando Cortez, a Marine early for a rendezvous with friends. Had a legit ID to back up that name as well."

"But his real name is?"

"Orlan Rebelo. Former Army EOD. Currently same post as Bredon at the agency."

"With a name like that we probably should've suspected him sooner, eh? Nice work. Why didn't you tell me any of this sooner?"

"I didn't put the pieces together until I found his personnel file. All I had was a face in a drugged haze I thought I'd seen elsewhere recently. It all sort of came together from there."

"Ok, you've convinced me with your impressive investigative skills. Now how do we find the guy?"

"I have an idea about that as well. It'll involve that hacker friend of yours. There's also something in his service record that caught my attention; he has a bone to pick with the intelligence community. I'll fill you in between catastrophes."

Chapter Fifteen: Stakeout

I can't believe I let you talk me into this," Divana said. Her seat was reclined and her eyes half closed, yet she was complaining for the third, or possibly fourth, time since Hal parked his National company vehicle on a quiet, residential street.

"I don't remember twisting your arm," he said.

"What, and let you get all the glory?"

"Glory? We're watching a guy's house, and we'll leave as soon as we verify his whereabouts."

"You do know there's drones designed *specifically* for this type of work. You do know that, right?"

"I've heard of them," said Hal. "Perhaps you'd like to give the DIA Director a call and tell him of their existence… or loan me some of yours."

"Nah. I'd rather whine to you about it; easier that way. Speaking of easy, appreciate you cleaning up the car for me. I like what you've done with the place."

"My car is always this clean. You know how fastidious I am, constantly picking up after you slobs. If you were all crooks instead of Marines, the cops would've caught you in about five minutes by following the trash trail."

"I remember," Divana said sleepily. "I'm just making conversation. It pleases me that you still get riled up over the same things."

Hal didn't respond. He busied himself with the display on his dash so he didn't have to see her smug smile or she see his grin. He rechecked the ping data Akeylah helped them obtain, to make sure they were watching the correct address, then he reviewed the limited vehicle data his car was set to automatically check for and something caught his attention. A car sitting on the opposite side and down the lane several homes came back as a government vehicle, and not the one assigned to Rebelo.

"Hey, we might have some company with the same idea as us," said Hal. "That car over there, look familiar to you?"

Divana sat up and rubbed the sleep from her eyes. She squinted and leaned forward, thinking the extra few inches would make a difference. "It's still dark out; this street isn't well lit, but it could be the car that DIA guy was picked up in outside Kettner. He tried to warn me off pursuing Bredon's case. What was his name? Mosin. Arkady Mosin."

Hal looked at her wide-eyed. "Mosin? He's Bredon's boss. We might have an ally in this manhunt."

"Or we might have an additional accomplice to take down. Just because he's not on your list doesn't mean he isn't involved."

That reminded him that he hadn't yet checked on the flagged list's user ID. He logged into the Agency database and punched in the number from the screenshot. He stared at it in disbelief for a moment before nudging Pris to point out the results.

"Ok, he created the list. So what?"

"I dunno," said Hal. "Let's go ask him."

He maneuvered the car alongside the other so the driver's windows were next to each other. As if on que, they both lowered their windows halfway and stared down one another.

"Supervisor Mosin," Divana said. "What brings you here on this fine evening?"

"Special Agent Pris. I should've guessed you'd do the exact opposite of what I asked."

"You really should've. Nevertheless, I'm here for official reasons as part of a criminal investigation. That can't be the reason you're here; you don't do criminal investigations."

"And what gives you that idea?"

It was Hal's turn to speak he figured. "Because you're the boss of the tactical to practical folks of Defense Intelligence. You flagged a list of names, many of whom are in your division. That list however is going to be considerably smaller when the sun comes up. You've tracked one of the few people still alive and out of custody; possibly the same way we did, and are trying to confirm his location, just like we are."

"I see," Arkady conceded. "Strange, you don't look like Anessa Kynes. She's the only person, aside from myself, who has happened across my list in recent days."

"It must be what I've done with my hair," Hal deadpanned. "How about you tell us the purpose of your list. Maybe we can anticipate the remaining members' next move, or flush out others you may have missed."

"I don't even know who you are. I see no reason to tell you anything."

"You do know who I am though," said Divana. "I should arrest you right now for treason and conspiracy, except my friend here seems to think you're not with that group who hijacked a dangerous satellite network. How about that for an incentive to cooperate?"

"I see your point. Since it's starting to feel like coming here was a ruse, how about we go somewhere and I'll tell you what I know over some coffee?"

"Finally, something I want to do," Divana quipped as they came around to follow behind Mosin.

~

That's it? That's the whole story?" Divana asked after downing the rest of her second cup of coffee. They sat in a booth of a mostly empty Lestat's Café on Park Street, not far from where they were staked out, just in case Rebelo's tapped mobile started to move. It was a quaint place; no expense wasted on excess decoration or opulent comfort. The graveyard shift staff knew their way around an espresso machine as well, which was what they all really needed at that moment.

"Correct Agent Pris," Arkady said. "It started out as a few people who had complaints of missing equipment leveled against them, which ballooned into a group of… I don't use this term lightly, terrorists."

"And you sent Bredon Fitzroy to investigate these allegations of theft?" Hal asked. "Why didn't you do it yourself?"

"As it was so eloquently pointed out, I'm not an investigator. But he was, in his past life; a good one by all accounts. Plus, it would be too obvious if I handled it personally, so I decided to delegate."

"So how do you account for him being tied to a chair and all?" said Divana. "He probably thought you'd double-crossed him; I'm still not convinced you haven't either. And what about the leak to the ATF?"

"I proposed the involvement to an outside agency; he felt the ATF was the most appropriate. Regarding his discovery, I'm still trying to figure it out myself. Could be a multitude of different ways."

"One of those ways being you told your buddies in that crooked outfit of yours where to find Bredon once his usefulness had ended?"

Hal gave Divana an unnerving look but she wasn't paying him any attention. She was in her interrogation mode and laser-focused on her suspect. Arkady on the other hand did something neither expected; he began to cry.

"You're right," he said after a sniffle. "To think that something like this couldn't happen right under my nose is peak hubris. I was too slow to respond, and when I got the courage to finally take action people started dying. After that, it was time to cover my ass until everything could be sorted. I hoped it had been cleared up at Miramar, then saw some activity from Rebelo and decided to follow him."

Hal wanted to give the guy a handkerchief or something. Problem was he didn't have one and Pris would probably grab it before the guy could use it anyway. "What sort of activity?" he asked instead.

"Um," another sniffle, "he was chatting with someone on a secure thread called 'Dir4' or something and his mobile was on the move. I went to where it last pinged and saw nothing until you two showed up."

"He used his government computer to chat somebody up?" Divana asked.

"No, it was a personal device. Once something connects to our network it can be monitored almost anywhere. It's not a widely advertised feature, though a similar setup can probably be found in nearly every government office."

Hal and Divana traded glances, both reflecting how private their personal lives really were. Neither considered themselves very careful when it came to their online footprint; home and work do overlap eventually no matter the undertaking to prevent it. To be reminded of how accessible data is even for officers of the state was a disconcerting experience for them. Wanting to change the subject, Hal was next to speak up.

"What was discussed on this… what was it called again?"

"I think Dir4. Don't know what that means but it basically went: 'everything's gone to hell, need to go to ground.' 'It can still be salvaged if we get the key back.' 'Do you know who has it?' 'One of yours; sandy hair, tan jacket, 40s…'"

"Wait a minute," Divana interrupted. "Dir4? Directive Four? That's why those NRO nutjobs thought they knew what they're talking about. They started their own group and named it after the thing they thought would protect them!"

"What the hell is Directive Four?" Hal asked.

"I'm genuinely relieved you don't know, so this stupid thing may eventually die out. It's an unwritten rule between federal agencies to not detain someone under investigation unless they're actually being arrested. Cops call it professional courtesy; I guess the feds wanted to be all MI6 about it. D4 used to be an investigator only thing, before my time. It has since bled into *all* corners of government."

"Sounds redundantly superfluous to me," said Mosin.

Both stared at him as if they'd forgotten he was there, then Divana said "It is, because if you're dirty and there's evidence of it, no rule, written or otherwise, is going to protect you from me."

Arkady visibly recoiled at her words, withered by the palpable contempt in her voice. Hal struggled once again to get them back on track.

"Do you have any idea who Rebelo was chatting with? Were there any screennames or identifiers to track down?"

"No names, just numbers and comments. However, I did get the distinct impression he was talking to a woman."

"What gave you that idea?" Divana asked, sounding a bit offended.

"Just the tone of the messages and the choice of words. I'm on my second wife and it sounded like my ex's gentle yet condescending voice. And the way she described someone using features a woman is more likely to point out… I think so anyway."

"What was that description again?"

"Sandy hair, tan jacket, 40s. I'm pretty sure she used the term 'dad bod' as well."

Pris rolled her eyes and looked at Hal. "She's talking about you, dummy. Great, now I'm saying 'she'."

"Me? I don't have a dad bod."

"Are you kidding? You could be the poster boy for dad bods! The question is who have you been around that knew you had the… oh crap."

Divana called one of her agents, despite it still being pre-dawn. "Takashi; figured you'd be awake. Who did we leave behind to hold down the fort when we went to Miramar? Uh-huh. Got it. Did she report anything when we got back? Oh yeah! I'll check the log. Thanks."

She hastily opened her folding tablet and rapidly maneuvered through several windows until she found what she was looking for. She read through a few times then her head sank, banging lightly on the table that smelled like dirty dishcloth.

"That by the book little… Listen to this: 'suspect A. Patel demanded she be allowed to speak to her attorney after being in custody for nearly ten hours. After threatening a lawsuit over her Sixth Amendment rights she was allowed access to a phone unsupervised for five minutes. She relinquished the phone after four minutes, twenty-six seconds but had erased the call log and data history. When asked why she did that she claimed it was an accident.'"

"Unsupervised? Where do you get these people?" Hal asked.

"That's what you're concerned about? Not that she's been playing us since the beginning?"

"Us? I've hardly spoken to her! I was getting ready to drag you out of that office in Coronado, leaving her behind to become part of the scenery."

"Do you want me to leave you two alone for a while?" Arkady said, receiving angry stares in response.

"I've gotta get back to the office, maybe get some answers out of her," Divana said after a prolonged pause. "Drop me at home so I can get cleaned up?"

Hal nodded and turned his attention to Mosin. "How can we get ahold of you if we need to, or visa versa?"

Arkady sent them both his contact information and said he'll be following Rebelo's phone like he was before.

"Can't we track via his online activity as well?"

"We can," Mosin said, "if he's active long enough to triangulate."

"Well then, we'll just have to get him online somehow," Divana said with a devious grin.

~

After dropping Pris off and speeding away in a hurry to escape her overprotective dogs, he had gone home, taken a quick shower, and decided to rest his eyes for an hour or so. The instant his head hit the pillow he was out and in a deep sleep. He woke up to his son, Sean, poking him with increasing ferocity by each jab.

"Can you take me to school dad?"

"What were you doing that made you miss your bus young man?" Hal asked groggily.

"Mom told me to miss the bus so you didn't sleep too late."

"Ah. Remind me to thank her when I clear up what I'm doing."

"What *are* you doing, besides sleeping on the couch for some reason? Anything to do with that gunfight at Miramar Airfield? Were you there?"

Hal looked at his growing boy with pride and empathy. He was certain if their roles were reversed, he'd want to know if their parents were doing something exciting as well.

"I was but I'm ok and I'm afraid if I tell you any more all your friends will know about it by lunchtime." Still half asleep, Hal realized he was nearly dressed when his stomach growled so loudly it made their cat growl back. Taming his inner beast would have to wait however.

"Mom trusts me to talk about her work," Sean said trying to play devil's advocate.

"She trusts you with *some* things that won't get her, or you, into trouble. There are other areas of her work she can't even tell *me* about, and my job is the same way. Look, I know how you feel; I'm still a very curious person too, but some of the information your mom and I are entrusted with can be dangerous if too many people know about it. I promise to tell you all about it when I'm allowed to, if you're still interested by then."

Sean begrudgingly accepted that response, for the moment at least, and they sped off toward his preparatory school so he didn't receive what would be his first tardy notice if he was late. Hal was still running on automatic; the events of the previous day firmly vying for his attention. Hugging his son goodbye brought him back to reality, and the realization he was missing a piece of the puzzle.

Back in his National and headed to the Navy base, he kept reaching out to his dash to dial up Pris yet stopping himself. If the infinity key was still useful to their cause, then Rebelo must've taken something from that home in San Francisco he could use it with. He connected a call through his onboard comms system except not to Pris, to Detective Calhoun of the San Francisco Police.

"Jon! Hal again. Sorry to bother you so early. I was able to identify the suspect in that Stanton

Avenue murder. Name's Orlan Rebelo; former Army explosives expert and currently with Defense Intelligence. Turns out we need to find him as well, in relation to that show last night."

Jon stared back in shock a few moments before responding. "Wow. Not sure which to address first; you practically solving a case for me or learning something the whole world is trying to find more information on. Either way it's not a bother at all!"

"Wish I could tell you more; probably said too much already. However, the woman who was killed used to be part of a team who built satellites for the Defense Department. There must've been a reason our man, Rebelo, went there. Has anything been reported missing?"

"Got a full inventory just last night," said Jon. "As far as the next of kin can tell, only one thing was stolen: a first-generation uplink coupler. Quite a mouthful. Apparently, she designed the thing and kept one for posterity, amongst some of her other achievements."

"That's *really* specific. Was someone else in the family an engineer who can explain how it works?"

"I can do you one better. She kept all of the schematics of everything she designed. If you can make heads-or-tails out of it I'll send you a copy, just don't get any ideas of stealing the design; the patent number is on every page."

"I could probably figure it out, given time. I know a guy who can take a look at it and tell me everything I need to know. Thanks Jon, we'll catch him," Hal said and disconnected.

There were strict guidelines about flying your vehicle in urban and residential areas, but he considered this an emergency and took off back to Skunk Works.

Chapter Sixteen: Mirage

Divana Pris wanted to punch the smug woman across the desk from her. She refrained, for the moment, because she knew Takashi, who was sitting in with her on the interview, either noticed this impulse and planned to stop her or was preparing to report her for striking a suspect... or both.

Akeylah Patel played dumb for a little while, though once her secure chatroom was revealed the remainder of her responses became "no comment."

"Very clever of you gaining some goodwill with us first to better facilitate getting what you want. I wonder, what's waiting for you in the colonies that you were so eager to get to?"

"No comment," she repeated after a prolonged silence, followed by a sheepish grin.

Back in her office, with the door closed, Divana paced the room like a caged animal. She debated calling the deputy director but didn't know what to say to him; unknown whereabouts of the infinity key and no ideas on its next planned use. She attempted to calm herself down and look at the situation logically:

If they were still seeking the same goal of reciprocity, then Rebelo wouldn't need to go somewhere with more than average access to aerospace assets. Their original plan was in total shambles now, so she doubted that could be a reliable strategy. The next step could very well be to make good on their threats, or an escalation into ransom territory.

She collapsed into her desk chair, drained from the events of the last few days, and frustrated that they're still ongoing without any identifiable direction. She was so deep in thought she almost missed an incoming call from a blocked number.

"Yeah," she answered.

"Good morning to you too," Hal said.

"Oh, Dune. Where the hell have you been? You sleep in or something?"

"As a matter of fact I did, just not as late as you think. I was able to see Sean a little this morning; dropped him off at school, then I followed up a lead with my secret squirrel."

"You do know that term was created for spies, right? Military intelligence? It doesn't encompass *everyone* who handles top secret stuff," she said.

"I am aware, thank you professor. Since I was going to see people at Skunk Works I wanted to go with a rodentia theme."

"Clever. Where are these rodents leading you?"

"Grab your coat and step outside, I'll be there in a few minutes. I'll explain on the way... after a quick indulgence."

~

They stopped at a drive-through for breakfast on their way east out of town. Hal said very little until he had a full stomach, which seemed to help Divana focus as well. Stress and sleep deprivation wears a person down sooner or later, but nutrition can often make or break that combination. With the city well behind them, Hal finally felt ready to let Divana weigh in on his plan, mainly due to the fact he had passed his point of no return.

"I know where Rebelo is going," he said. "Or at least what his next move will be."

"Ok. Is there a reason why you couldn't tell me this before leaving civilization?"

"Because you would've insisted on a full tactical unit or some advance team and I didn't want to spook him."

"We're not the CIA, Dune," said Pris. "I don't have a spy network I can just activate at a moment's notice. Besides, he already knows what you look like; probably me too. What advantage are the two of us supposed to have?"

"The advantage that one car is less conspicuous than several and he doesn't know we're on to him. I've also left my tan macintosh at home, so I'm less immediately recognizable."

"That'll make all the difference I'm sure," Divana said sarcastically. "So what popular tourist destination are you taking me to now?"

"Rice Airfield. It was an Army Air Corps base during World War II, built in the Mojave Desert to train pilots for the African Campaign. The Army handed it over to civilian control shortly after the War ended, and it was completely abandoned sometime in the late 1950s. About a century later, someone restored it and turned it into a museum focusing primarily on history of air and space combat, calling on retired experts in the field to contribute."

"Out of all the questions I have, I'm going with 'how does a museum in the middle of nowhere stay in business and who would fund such a thing?'"

Hal looked over at her quizzically. "If those are the things you want to know you can ask on the tour. *We're* going there because Rebelo needs a piece of old tech currently on display at the museum, to connect with something he stole from a residence in San Francisco."

Hal summarized the theft and death of Ania Mishima, then what Elwin Koehl described about what an uplink coupler would likely need to connect with satellites. She listened without comment, furrowing her brow occasionally when confused. Once he'd finished, Pris remained silent for a moment while Hal accelerated and entered a sky lane that had recently formed.

"And this museum is the only place he can find a... whatever thingy to connect to his uplink coupler?" she asked, finally working out his plan.

"First of all, it's called a transponder with isotropic modulator, or TIM. And secondly the museum is the only place he can be sure to find one on short notice. It's possible he knows of a private collector or something like the coupler, which would be unfortunate for us. A working TIM however is listed on the museum's website. The thing shows up there on a basic search for it."

"Almost like someone is sending a message. Seems a little convenient to me, like we're being led somewhere... or away."

"That's possible," said Hal, "although I think the convenience is for Rebelo's sake. The completed device, along with the infinity key, will need a powerful transmitter and access to specific software that you can't find just anywhere. As it happens, there's another airfield set up during World War II nearby that has those things."

"Great. Yes, I love it when a plan comes together. And since I know you're dying to tell me about this other place, go ahead and get it off your chest now."

"Thanks, I think, but there's not much else to say. Other than it already existing as an airfield, Blythe has a very similar background as Rice, plus it somehow managed to stay open as an airport."

"And this airport in the desert has the necessary equipment to connect with ODIN?" Divana asked, her skepticism beginning to return a little.

"There's some privately owned buildings in an unused part of the property that do, I'm told. The Army had expanded farther than the civilian airport needed, so some of the infrastructure was left to rot, until around the same time as Rice Airfield Museum was established."

"Where are you getting this from? Is your source on this reliable?"

"He asked me not to identify him but yes, it's from my secret squirrel. He also tipped me off on where to look for who owns those buildings at Blythe: Muroc Ventures Unlimited. I did a little digging… very little to be honest, and found that Muroc is the former name of Edwards Air Force Base. The company is on a Defense Department contract."

Pris nodded yet said nothing and turned her head to stare out the window. Nothing except blue skies and tan dunes as far as the eye could see. A bleak, mostly featureless landscape rushing by in a blur. The car's instruments however indicated a slight change in scenery coming up soon, with a few scattered hills. Beyond those was their destination. Hal gained a little more altitude to compensate, as instructed by the onboard navigation system. His speed was also increased, though not because it was considerately suggested to him by an algorithm; he suddenly become apprehensive about missing their target.

~

They touched down on the old, refurbished runway of Rice Airfield. It was the same size and chevron-shaped patch of black concrete as it was while in active use, except now there was an array of solar cells protecting vehicles and patrons from the harsh desert sun.

The place was fairly busy for a Thursday morning. There were school transports and private vehicles in equal numbers. Rice Museum had only just opened for the day a short time ago and eager children, accompanied by dour adults, crowded around the tram pickup area like a bustling ant colony.

Divana and Hal casually surveyed the crowd for their target, Orlan Rebelo, and were getting a little anxious when they couldn't find him.

"Could he have come yesterday?" she asked, doubt prevalent in her voice.

"The place was closed before we raided Miramar and he stole the infinity key, he couldn't have known he needed to before then. Plus, I hope the museum would publicize the theft of a piece of technology they advertise."

That didn't seem to appease her uncertainty but she didn't press. Instead, she took another look at the crowd, forming tidy lines to enter the tram. Showing no concern for discomfort she stood between the two queues and looked into the eyes of all adults. Both she and Hal took up the end of the line and the tram gently pulled away toward the museum.

It was a parched and desolate place. On the other hand, great care was taken to replicate how the old air base looked, within reason of course. Only so much you could do quite literally in the middle of nowhere. An automated presentation was playing, providing historical tidbits and black-and-white photos of the base in its heyday. What caught Divana's attention however was the announcement stating they were indeed on the first tram of the day. She began to formulate a plan for surveillance when something at the main building caught her attention.

"Could we have gone straight to the museum since this is technically police business?" she asked pointing toward a small staff parking lot with several vehicles.

"I didn't ask. Thought it better to blend in and catch him unaware," he responded.

"Well, just in case, have your autopilot park the car as close to the emergency area as you can. We'll fill security in when we get there."

Hal programmed his National to arrive at the main museum a few minutes after them, and turned on its transponder which contained codes to recognize it as law enforcement vehicle. Once finished, he stepped off the tram with Divana, ahead of the school children, and instantly understood how the place could remain open given its location.

The Rice Airfield Museum wasn't so much a historical account of desert air combat as it was a love letter to aviation and aerospace throughout the ages. Everywhere he looked there were interactive displays where you could build engines and design aircraft. The most popular however, and most enticing to Hal, was the many flight simulators, which covered some of the first aircraft up to just before the most recent War. The vast majority of school children were crowded around there. Hal found himself drifting that direction as well, until his movement was stopped by a firm grasp on his elbow.

"No time to play," said Divana. "We have to talk to security before they deactivate our ride." A few tugs on his arm got him moving the other direction while he saved the location on his mobile to remind him to bring Sean here.

The security office, which was little more than an alcove by the staff entrance, was occupied by one man who Hal guessed was retired military by his bored yet vigilant demeanor. He begrudgingly allowed Hal to keep his car in the emergency spot, though warned it would be immediately moved for real emergency vehicles.

"Copy," said Hal. "We don't think it will come to that. We're here to prevent a theft. Can you tell us where this item is?" He showed the man in the starched uniform an image of the TIM from his folding tablet. A crease formed across the man's forehead as he deliberated for a few seconds.

"Ah, yes. That's in our Orbital section. Somebody wants to steal that? What for? It doesn't have any tangible value."

"Is what you have on display the real thing or a replica?" Divana asked, ignoring the guard's questions.

"We have some replicas out for public interaction but that's not one of them since, as I said, it has no value. Plus, security was recently upgraded in that section; there's a techie working on it right now in fact."

Hal and Divana exchanged glances then took off running in the direction of what they thought was the orbital section. They narrowly avoided collisions with school children and stopped to consult a map. The museum wasn't big but there were a lot of side rooms and hallways that could become confusing quickly.

Orbital was the opposite corner from the security station. They were headed in the right direction after all and nearly there, so they took the last quarter of the building more calmly to draw less attention and better prepare their senses for a quick response.

Hal and Divana guardedly entered the quiet and less frequented area of the museum that covered near space technologies. There were no simulator games or interactive knowledge centers here, just plain and simple historical tidbits and items. A model of the first space station rotated silently above their heads, which mesmerized Hal until he received a nudge from Pris.

It took them only a few seconds of searching in that relatively small space until they found what brought them there. The polished name plate next to it read:

Transponder with Isotropic Modulator (TIM)

Donated by: Ania Mishima of San Francisco

It was locked safely behind plexiglass but they weren't taking any chances.

"Yo, can you unlock Cabinet 47, Lot 9 for a quick inspection?" Divana asked the security guard via a well-hidden intercom. There was a soft click as the door popped open barely enough to access. Hal nudged it the rest of the way and reached for the device. All he grabbed was sanitized air.

"Damn, it's a hologram."

Divana mashed the intercom controls more forcefully now. "Where is that security technician? Is he still on the premises?"

There was a short pause, then his gravelly voice returned saying he was just leaving the tech room on the corner adjacent to them. Hal closed the door on the facsimile and they ran back across the crowded central room.

Hal and Divana made it only partway through the throng of children in the central area when they caught a glimpse of a man in workman's jumpsuit down a side hallway. The pair slowed and fell in behind the man at a distance too far to make a positive identification.

While their target never looked around nervously, like the average person who has done something wrong would, Divana spotted a few things that increased her assurance they were following the right person. For one thing, he walked like a soldier. With all the marching, running, and drills in formation service members subconsciously learn to move with a certain confidence, and this man fit that style perfectly.

Next was the work coveralls he was wearing. They were new and still had the creases indicating they were unfolded very recently. She could also tell the boots were broken in but had a shine almost worthy of parade gloss.

Those combined with the fact he still hadn't turned around convinced her that she should make that conclusive identification. "Orlan Rebelo," she yelled down the short hallway.

The man froze mid-step and stood motionless while Hal held his breath. Then, almost impossibly fast, he spun and fired twice with a weapon neither saw him reach for.

Divana was quicker to react, pushing Hal one direction of the hallway while she dove the other. Hal practically bounced off the wall and had his own sidearm out when he recovered. Rebelo was nowhere to be seen. She was down on one knee, her weapon out as well. Neither had any obvious injuries, and checking behind them there didn't appear to be any bystanders hit either. The gunfire however didn't go unnoticed.

Pandemonium began to spread through the museum like a wave. The excited voices of play and awe were gradually being replaced by cries of indistinctive panic. The children looked to be handling the situation better than their adult chaperones, who were fretfully herding them back to the tram stop.

Aside from the increased noise, the situation was a welcome benefit for Hal and Divana because they now had an unimpeded path to security and the employee parking lot. They picked up their pace however when rounding the corner toward security. The guard lay on the floor in front of the exit doors, blood soaking into the cheap beige carpet that was glued directly to the concrete floor.

"He's hit! The bastard shot him," said Hal. "See if there's a kit at his workstation or something."

Pris leapt into the closet that held the security station. After a few seconds of rummaging, she emerged with a grey toolbox with red crosses made by electrical tape adorning the top. Hal opened the box and was relieved at how well stocked it was. There were a few items out of date, he noticed, though still safely useable.

"Do we really have time for this?" she asked quietly. "Rebelo is getting away."

"This man is still alive, and I'm going to make sure he stays that way until the medics get here. Besides, we know where Rebelo is going anyway. To speed things up maybe you can call to make sure paramedics are actually on their way."

Divana wanted to protest, but decided he was probably right. In group mentality there's always the assumption somebody else has already called for help, when in fact nobody has. She also wasn't sure injuries had been reported, so she called while Hal worked his magic. His movements were practiced and efficient, wasting nothing of available supplies or time.

By the time she disconnected the call Hal had patched up the entry and exit wounds, after cleaning off the area to assess the damage. He worked quickly and proficiently. Divana had been around him while he dealt with similar injuries after, even during, a firefight yet had never actually watched him work. She now completely understood why her unit lost the fewest people during the war out of all the Marine infantry.

"Ok," Hal said talking to the security guard, "you had a through-and-through. I've stopped the bleeding so you should be fine if you get to a proper surgery center and replenish your fluids within the hour. I didn't use the morphine patch you smuggled in your kit; didn't want to risk altering your heartbeat or anything. Now that you're not leaking anymore do you want it? Are you in a lot of pain?"

The man's breathing had stabilized while Hal was talking to him. He still looked pale however, and seemed like he could pass out at any moment. Hal was about to apply the patch when the man waved him off.

"I'll be alright," he said in a voice even gravellier than before. "Just don't let the sonofabitch who shot me get away! He was driving a white utility van with a blue logo on the side; a globe or sun or something," he concluded with a pained cough.

Hal was reluctant to leave but the man kept gesturing toward the doors. He placed an electrolytic drink next to him and held out an auto-doc personal IV and said "drink this now, slowly: a sip every thirty seconds or so. If they're still not here by the time you finish put this on your left forearm, just below the elbow. Got it?"

"Yeah, copy. Now get out of here before the ambulance arrives and your car gets disabled and automatically moved out of the way."

Hal nodded and Pris practically dragged him outside. Once they were in the car though they headed due south as fast as the vehicle would take them; the injured security guard now seemingly a distant memory.

Chapter Seventeen: The Chase

To close some ground on their quarry, Hal gained as much altitude as his National would let him. Warnings and alarms were lighting up his dash saying they were too high and going too fast. He did his best to silence or ignore them all but several would persistently return after a few seconds. When the car's shuddering got too much for them, he took them down to a lower altitude for his equilibrium to compensate.

"That should buy us a little time, and still get us there in one piece," said Hal.

"And you're sure Blythe is where he's going?"

"You've already asked me that. No, not sure, however the next closest place he can uplink to ODIN is over two hours away, at Edwards Air Force Base. Blythe is both closer and easier to access."

"I guess you were right the first time," Divana admitted. "Now that Rebelo is sufficiently spooked, do you see any reason why we can't call in the calvary now?"

Hal gave her a look as if she'd just said something insane. "You can call everyone you think of. One problem though… who would be able to respond in a useful timeframe?"

"I don't know, but we need to call *somebody*. We don't know what Rebelo's plan is exactly and nobody knows where we are or why we're out here."

Hal made a noncommittal noise and she made the call. Since he was usually alone when in the field it didn't occur to him to give someone a status update; he had his backup sitting next to him. This wasn't a routine site visit or inspection; the stakes were much higher and they needed all the help they could get. He turned on his radio, set it to the general civilian band, and decided to make a call as well.

"Blythe Tower, this is government vehicle 742 Charlie, come in please." Silence. Not even static. Hal was about to repeat his call for the third time when a tired voice came on the channel.

"This is Blythe. What can we do for you 742 Charlie."

"Blythe, 742 has federal agents in pursuit of an armed suspect who might be heading to the private property at the edge of your airfield. We are requesting a police response."

"Copy 742. To ensure appropriate response, what is this person suspected of, and travelling in?"

"Suspect is Orlan Rebelo. He's wanted for murder in San Francisco and attempted murder of a security guard at Rice Museum. Last seen in a light-colored utility van with a blue logo on the side."

"Understood 742. We'll make the call. In the future feel free to simply use the phone; this frequency is typically reserved for aircraft, over."

Hal made no response and looked over to see Divana smiling at him. "You already knew that didn't you?" she asked, shaking her head. "You just wanted to use the radio." He shrugged and looked for something to change the subject. Fate, it seemed, was on his side.

"Do you see that dust cloud up ahead?" Hal asked. Pris squinted out the windshield then gave up and switched on the forward camera view, maximum magnification.

"Now I do. How the hell did you see that?"

"Eyesight hasn't failed me yet," he said. "Looks like we might be able to catch him before he reaches Blythe."

"That's good news. Have you given any thought as to *how* we're going to catch him? Does this thing have any offensive capabilities?"

"It's got an electromagnetic pulse emitter and some communication jamming tags. That's about it. Defensively there's chaff grenades and flares. Not sure how that will help us though."

"That'll have to do," she said. "Can this thing estimate time to intercept a moving target?"

Hal manipulated a few menus on his onboard computer and a timer appeared on the heads-up display. "Looks like we'll intercept a few minutes before we reach the airfield."

The minutes ticked away. There was so little change in the landscape that it seemed like they weren't moving at all, aside from the dust trail in front of them progressively becoming larger. Eventually, detail on the vehicle kicking up the sand began to emerge and they could confirm it was a white utility van.

With some exceptions, most vans of the type they were chasing could neither gain a higher altitude nor accelerate very fast. Given their target was traveling on the public road at close to the speed limit, Hal assumed it wasn't an upgraded version.

"So, what's the plan?" Divana asked. "I was thinking we zap him with the EMP and pull in front of the car in case he has an override."

"Sounds good. The EMP has a decent range but I'll close to ten meters, just to be sure."

Despite all the dust and dirt it was disturbing, the van could be clearly seen through the windscreen. Hal began to drop to an attack posture, matching speed and charging the EMP. The van took no evasive action, despite the high likelihood Rebelo would have seen them by now.

"Firing EMP on three," said Hal. "Three!"

Nothing happened. The utility van didn't waiver in the slightest. All the instruments indicated the pulse fired, there was simply no visible effect.

"Do you want to try again? Maybe get over the top of him this time," Divana said.

Hal repositioned over the top of the van and tried to disrupt the electrical systems a second time with the EMP. Same result. Hal slumped back in his seat in a huff.

"Damn thing must be shielded. Guess we'll have to just follow him in."

Pris began to say something but was cut off by a staccato beeping from the car. The collision alarm. She glanced up to the windscreen and couldn't believe her eyes; large pieces of the van were peeling off and flying directly at them. Hal swerved right, then left, then tried to fly over the debris until a chunk of the van's front fender struck the National's undercarriage, instantly effecting their ability to maintain altitude.

Out of the remains of the utility van sprang a black Yeager-class scout craft. It was out of their visual range in seconds traveling at near supersonic speed. Hal and Divana watched it disappear in utter shock, unable to form words.

"The primary field generator has been damaged," Hal said, finally finding his voice. "We're running at about half power. I can either push it to try and keep up, possibly stranding ourselves out here, or take it easy and hope the locals catch him before we get there."

"Would it help if we turned off everything we don't need right now? Whatever gets us there in one piece as quickly as possible is my answer by the way, so don't feel compelled to ask again."

"Thanks," Hal muttered as he began shutting down unnecessary systems, and a few useful ones. "Didn't give us much but I'll risk adding some more speed... mostly because I turned off the air conditioning as well."

~

They travelled in silence. The only sound that could be heard was the struggling of the car's motors, and the occasional ping from Pris's mobile when they passed every two miles on her map. They were still five minutes away yet they could already see the smoke.

Two columns of black smoke coiled up to the cloudless sky, and they soon traced the cause of the fires. They approached two ruined Riverside County Sheriff cruisers that looked like they were hit by precision weapons fire. The damage they saw before them could've been caused by any number of armaments a Yeager was known to carry, though the most likely candidate was mini-missiles as it was the most common.

Hal instinctively slowed to check for survivors. He saw no movement or signs of life yet still felt the urge to stop. Divana grabbed his arm.

"We can't help them, Dune. Even if they're still alive, which doesn't look promising, they'll need a little more than a Band-Aid. We're close to the airport; let's call it in and prevent Rebelo from killing more people."

Hal gritted his teeth as they passed the mangled husks that once were police interceptors. While Pris called in the scene's location, the structures of Blythe began to take shape on the horizon. Before long he could make out where the airfield lay and where they needed to go.

To call Blythe Airfield small would be an understatement. It remained operational due to private aircraft owners, a school for flying lessons, and stipends from multiple state and nonprofit donors. Despite all that, due to the extreme heat and wind the place was in dire need of renovation.

Paint was faded and cracked. Tinting on the windows was peeling off like old wallpaper. The roof for one of the hangars was about to collapse. The contrast of that image made locating the much newer, and better funded, communications center far easier than Hal expected.

The building was relatively small. It was a windowless, characterless box that looked to be surrounded on all sides with solar panels. There was a slightly larger warehouse-type building next door, connected by a covered parking area, big enough to accommodate three vehicles. The scout craft was there listing to one side, possibly due to ramming through the formidable gate, or the defensive position a third Riverside County cruiser tried to maintain. The deputy this time however thankfully survived the intruder unharmed, unlike his vehicle and deployed web trap.

"Why didn't he find a more vulnerable part of the fence instead?" Divana asked.

"Not sure. Maybe the EMP had some effect on his ride after all."

They showed the bewildered deputy their credentials and proceeded through the mangled remains of the gate. The cruiser came to a lumbering halt into the carport, blocking the Yeager in as much as possible. Hal opened the door to exit but Pris stopped him.

"You're not just going to run in there and hope we shoot him before he shoots us, are you?"

"Do you have a better idea?"

"Yes, I think I might."

~

Hal and Divana cautiously entered the outer room of the glossy black building. It was cramped and dark with a couple lockers in one corner next to a sanitation station. The corner opposite the lockers was a small, open area, about the size of a single-person shower with a grated floor to brush off sand and dust before entering the next chamber, Hal speculated.

Divana nudged him then slapped something in his hand. He studied the device, rolling it over trying to determine the best way to hold it. Two cylindrical objects unevenly bound together by duct tape was her master plan to give them an offensive window of opportunity. In only about five minutes, Pris managed to turn the flares and chaff grenades from his car into an improvised disruption device.

"Are you sure this is going to work?" Hal asked with growing concern.

"For the third time, no; I'm not sure. If you had a flash-bang or concussion grenade I wouldn't have needed to MacGuyver these. It's this or nothing. Now get on the other side of the door and be ready to light your flare on my mark."

Hal inspected the device once more, finding the trigger she rigged up. He wasn't sure how she managed it in the few minutes of tinkering she had but her ingenuity might just save their lives. He took position opposite Pris and they lit their flares a couple seconds before she slapped the button to open the inner door.

The dark aperture was filled with a hail of gunfire. The shots were so rapid Hal imagined the man being subjected to electrotherapy while firing. Bright, midday sunlight was peeking through the outside from the fresh holes in the door, drastically increasing the light in the dim room. It was now or never, before Rebelo decided to walk right up to them in their partially blinded state.

Hal threw his contraption right and Divana left. They could be heard clattering on flooring panels, then seconds later a loud pop as the chaff exploded everywhere. An unexpected noise followed; a sharp gasp and pained cough. Between that and the stoppage of gunfire, they figured there wouldn't be a better time than now. Divana plunged into the next room with Hal close behind.

The room was square with wall-to-wall equipment and a single terminal in the center, not unlike a few other specific rooms they'd been to in recent days. Rebelo stood next to the terminal holding the left side of his face, and a very large pistol still firmly in his right hand. Divana wasted no time and commenced shouting commands. Either he didn't hear or chose to simply ignore her.

Then, as quickly as he moved back at the museum, raised his gun and resumed firing. The shots were wild, and Rebelo didn't get many off before Hal and Divana returned fire. Rebelo spun and fell like a rag doll. Hal quickly ran over and took the man's hand cannon, throwing it to the opposite corner of the room. When he turned around Pris was still in the same spot, holding her side.

"Bastard got a lucky shot off," she said through clenched teeth. "It grazed the edge of my armor. Looks worse than it is, apart from leaking like crazy."

Hal scanned the space for a first-aid kit, didn't find one, then searched the foyer where he found it above the refresh station. Checking its contents he sighed, seeing it wasn't going to be as useful as the one at the museum. This kit had dehydration and sunburns in mind when putting it together, though there was still some sterile gauze and a small tube of liquid skin sealant. A clotting spray would be extremely useful but this would have to do.

When he returned Pris had moved closer to Rebelo and moved him onto his back. "What were you doing?" he asked running over to them.

"What do you think? I'm checking him for more weapons. You know, for when he wakes up."

"Wakes up? You didn't use lethal rounds?"

"You did?" she shrieked, then flinched in pain.

"The guy has killed three people that we know of and tried to kill four more! Why is this even a question?" Hal said as he began tending to her gunshot wound.

Divana winced then resumed. "Weren't you the one who talked me out of using lethal force yesterday? Besides, I thought we might need him to stop or undo whatever it is he's doing here."

"Quit fidgeting, I'm almost done."

"Somehow, this both hurts and tickles."

"You're welcome." The bleeding stopped and the wound bandaged, Hal went back to the outer room to wash his hands. Upon returning Rebelo became his next patient. He wasn't breathing and the blood loss was severe. It was clear the man was dead. There were also several silvery slivers protruding from the skin on the left side of his face and neck.

Chaff was typically strips of aluminum dispersed over a wide area to confuse radar. One of their improvised disruption devices must've landed just right to be at least partially aimed in Rebelo's direction. It was a horrific sight, so much so that it made Hal turn away in revulsion.

"Hmm, you don't see *that* every day, do you Dune?" Pris quipped, equally disgusted about the sight. "Since our friend here can't tell us what he was up to we should probably try to figure it out, sooner rather than later."

"It's funny you think he would be helpful in any way given what he did to get to this point," Hal said as he sat down at the central terminal. Right away he recognized the two collected items attached and plugged into one of the ports with the infinity key sticking out the end. Then he studied the display and tried to figure out what it was telling him. The realization hit him like a punch to the gut.

"Well, that can't be good."

Chapter Eighteen: Ragnarök

"What? What did you do?" Divana asked, gingerly making her way over to see for herself. "Does that say what I think it does?"

"I'm not positive, but it looks like he set ODIN up to target the largest members of the intelligence community around the world. The lower tier satellites seem to be programmed to spread out and transmit a jamming signal as well, if I'm reading this right. They're still getting into position."

"This is some James Bond villain stuff right here! How will doing this help them gain notoriety among the other aerospace agencies?"

"My guess?" Hal began, "is this is meant to make the world blind and deaf, giving the biggest players a clean slate. If you recall from his service record, he blames the intel community for his friends being burned by agencies not sharing valuable information. An ironic but unsubtle punishment."

"Well, isn't that dandy. This point will also likely kill hundreds, if not thousands of people, and quite possibly start another war. How do we stop it?"

"I have no idea. I've been trying to shut it down but either it takes specific words and phrases, or Rebelo set up a passcode of some kind."

"The infinity key," Divana said. "How do we make it work?"

Hal looked over to the intricately designed cover for the drive, plugged into the TIM and uplink coupler, now remembering what its function was. "Good question. I'm open to suggestions. This isn't exactly a Fedora operating system like I'm used to."

Divana leaned over, holding her side, and started pushing buttons until she found what she was looking for. A menu appeared on the display and she alternated between looking at it and Hal.

"Maybe try external drive? That would be my guess," she said with a condescending pat on his shoulder.

Once he started navigating through the menu prompts, Hal began to understand how the system worked. It was simplicity to the extreme, programmed for single-word commands. He started with the word Status and a global display with highlighted dots was projected above the central workstation. A taskbar showed that optimal fire-control formation was at 47% and climbing.

"We're running out of time," he said.

"Then why don't you try CANCEL or SHUTDOWN?"

Hal entered Cancel and the status display disappeared. He tried a second time and nothing happened. Shutdown had the same result and he was beginning to get nervous.

"How the hell did Rebelo have time to program this all in?" said Hal. "There must've been this exact attack formation already in the system, we just have to figure out what it's called."

There was a series of loud noises coming from outside, despite the sound dampening walls of the building. It sounded like sirens followed by a mass closing of car doors. Only one way to find out.

"I'll go check that out, you keep trying. Maybe the answer is on him somewhere," Divana said kicking Rebelo's limp leg on her way out the door.

Hal ran over to the prone corpse. Most of the pooled blood had seeped through the removable floor panels by then. He tried not to imagine the awful mess that must be down there, amongst all the wires and fiber optics.

Emptying Rebelo's pockets revealed nothing of immediate interest. Hal searched through the man's mobile phone with mounting frustration. The phone had very few frills, much like his own. It would take time checking every application that allowed information to be manually entered; time he didn't have.

Although he'd never used it before, Hal tried the search feature of the phone; results were promising but it too would take time to review. A cramp was beginning to form in his lower back, most likely due to his poor posture seated on the floor. Hal decided instead to stand and pace the room while he perused the mobile and something caught his eye on the back of Rebelo's hand.

It was written in ink along the first joint of the left thumb. Hal couldn't recall the last time he'd seen ink, and a pen wasn't amongst the man's pocket contents. He didn't dwell on that oddity long because he raced the few paces over to the central terminal to enter the word PANDORA.

The display changed menus to a detailed list of options and data, rather than the merely summarized one from before. "Now we're talking." Hal said to himself and started searching for a way to kill Pandora.

~

Divana stepped back out into the blinding sunlight. Being in the dimness of the communication station it took her eyes a little extra time to adjust. Once they did, she was taken aback by the throng of activity that greeted her.

Countless police and emergency vehicles of all shapes and sizes filled the space between the small, fenced-in area containing the two buildings of the private communication outpost, and the quaint Blythe Airfield. From a few different types of cruisers to vans with SWAT emblazoned on the side, even a bomb squad truck or two sprinkled in for good measure, made up the sea of flashing lights before her. The impressive response wasn't what concerned her however, it was the fact most of the people in uniform had their guns pointed at her.

Divana raised her hands instinctively. She saw the futility in trying to talk over the din so she walked directly toward the vehicle they passed at the gated fence. This maneuver made some of the officers start shouting orders. She held out hope that by now her NCIS shield clipped to her belt would be clearly visible. Her law enforcement imbedded chip should be detectable as well.

She reached the front line of officers and said "Special Agent Divana Pris. Where is the deputy who was here a few minutes ago?"

The question caught the police pointing assault weapons at her off guard. A man with captain bars elbowed his way to the front and the phalanx of uniforms parted ways begrudgingly. "Seeking medical attention, Special Agent Pris. What is your business here on this property?"

"My *business*? Did the officers on scene make any statements? Did nobody contact the airport control tower about our call to them over a half hour ago?"

The captain cleared his throat ruefully and said "I haven't been fully briefed on the situation. All I know is a terrorist attack has been reported and it's being orchestrated from the building *you* just exited. The National Security Agency representative who reported this advised if we couldn't regain control within the next twenty minutes it would be targeted for an airstrike."

"Well tell whomever is giving you these scraps of information that the terrorist is dead and to call off the airstrike. Blowing up the building isn't going to undo what he did anyway. We're in the process of shutting it down; we just need the time to do it."

"Begging your pardon ma'am, but I'd like to see this for myself before making that call."

Divana curtsied aside and said "right this way then gentlemen. Hopefully my partner inside has the situation under control already. In any case, time is short if you're not going to take the word of a federal agent."

"No offense intended. I'm a firm believer of the philosophy of 'trust but verify.' Please lead the way, Agent Pris."

Divana spun and made for the black cube that was the private comms center. She caught a few glimpses in her peripheral vision to notice the police captain had gathered an entourage of six additional people, all SWAT members. She couldn't help but continue to feel slighted, though reckoned she might do the same thing if their roles were reversed.

The walk back seemed a lot longer than the trip to the fence line. As she approached the gleaming obsidian building a sense of dread began to grow within her. Not from the small army that had gathered around the perimeter, or the half dozen heavily armed people accompanying her. It was the proximity of the building itself. She knew she should be going the opposite direction, and silently hoped Hal had made some progress so they could do that very thing long before the deadline.

~

Hal's number of guesses of the magic word that would unlock the Pandora attack was somewhere in the high thirties when he heard, and felt, the woosh of the inner door opening. Without looking over he said "Good timing. I'm about ready to smash this thing and then track down anybody left who designed it to do the same. How's everything outside?"

"We have guests, Dune. What's your progress?" Divana responded, ignoring Hal's question.

He turned with a jerk to see Pris flanked by half a dozen people in full tactical gear and one man who looked like he was interrupted on his way to a press conference. "Welcome. Maybe you can help me think of a word to shut this thing down."

The newcomers all looked to Pris for clarification. She said "you haven't stopped it yet? Have you made any headway at *all*?"

"Our friend here had the name of the program written on his hand. I can now see the progress of the attack; I just can't seem to do anything about it. I'm thinking he locked access."

"Have you tried UNLOCK?" Divana asked.

Hal turned in his chair and entered the word. A new image appeared requesting a password. "Well, at least we can confirm he locked access, not sure how that helps us though."

An awkward silence permeated the space, causing the numerous fans and computations to seem louder than they were before. Several SWAT members began shifting their feet until finally the captain cleared his throat.

"Can someone fill me in as to what the target is? I don't believe that's been covered yet."

"Targets, plural Cap," said Divana. "And we're talking roughly a couple dozen of the largest spy organizations around the world. As you can see, blowing this place up won't solve that particular problem. In fact, I think this is the *only* place that can stop this thing. Can you please relay that message?"

The officer didn't respond. He took a few paces adjacent to Hal, looked around the room as if he were an appraiser attempting to estimate value, then walked back to where he was before. Pointing at the body on the floor he said "who's this?"

"Orlan Rebelo," Hal answered. "Rogue agent who put this doomsday scenario in motion… with some help. Now what's this about being blown up?"

"Oh sorry, didn't I mention that an airstrike, out of Edwards I presume, will be on us in about ten minutes. Unless of course we either stop the attack or it's called off by *someone* who convinces the Air Force not to proceed," Divana concluded, giving the police captain a pleading stare.

The officer put his hands up, relenting. "Message received Agent Pris. I'll step outside and request a standdown; I'm not getting a signal in here."

He departed the comms building, taking along most of his SWAT cadre; one remained in the room to watch them and relay information Hal guessed.

"Right, so what is our next move? Whether we bought ourselves an extra ten minutes or not really won't matter if we can't stop this."

Hal stood up and began stretching. He started with his neck, then moved to his shoulders and worked his way down to his feet in disciplined fashion. When he finished, he sat back down at the central terminal and resumed typing.

"Did that help you or was it just a way to ignore me?" Pris asked.

"It did actually; help I mean. I'm getting nowhere trying to stop the attack. How about I change the targets?"

"Change it to what? Is that something you think you can…" she trailed off as the display changed to a list of coordinates. She didn't recognize the locations, but the caption above them that read Target Assignment told her everything she needed to know.

"First guess," Hal said triumphantly. "Now, let's see if we can't get it to shoot at itself."

"Where are you going to get coordinates of moving, orbital objects?"

Hal pressed a few keys and the projected hologram of the Earth suddenly had numbers appear next to the floating yellow dots.

"Ok. Good teamwork. Shall I read off the numbers to you?"

"Please. Just make sure the pair have a clean line of sight to each other," Hal replied.

She was able to get several targets in when the door to the room burst open, admitting an out of breath police captain. He took a moment to regard Divana and Hal, then whispered something to the remaining SWAT officer, who promptly departed. He took a breath, bracing himself for the news.

"The Air Force refused to cancel the airstrike. Says they can't risk any more incursions from this location."

Hal stared at the man agape. Divana was incredulous. "But this is listed as private property. Someone with enough money and influence to build this place is the victim of a crime and the military is going to bomb it? If that doesn't scream coverup I don't know what does! Not to mention there's two federal agents inside."

"I explained all that," said the captain still slightly short of breath. "Which is why they allowed for extra time to evacuate the area. We now have less than fifteen minutes to be out of here."

Divana looked to Hal and said "is that going to be enough time?"

"It'll have to be. I don't want to die in a place that looks like a Rubik's Cube with all the colors taken off."

She turned to tell the captain to clear out, but all she saw was empty space. It was back to merely her, Hal, and Rebelo on the floor. "So, where did we leave off?"

"Um, seventeen; slightly over halfway done," Hal said and got back to entering telemetry data she relayed.

They were getting to the end of their list; with a few minutes to spare and something occurred to Divana. "What about all the other ODIN satellites? What's their role in Pandora?"

Hal looked at her as if she started speaking another language all of a sudden. Then realization crossed his face, and ultimately despondency. He finished entering the final targeting data, then entered the keyword of Status. A new countdown had begun for the assault satellites to acquire their new targets. When scrolling to the next page he let out an audible laugh.

"What is it?" Pris asked, stepping closer to the display.

"Seems the designers of ODIN, or maybe just Pandora, had a sense of irony. The defense satellites are programmed to protect the offensive ones from attack. Then, once the gods have punished us for our curiosity and hubris, they turn on each other until all strike satellites are destroyed."

"That's great professor, but what happens if they're already gone? Does that change anything?"

"I guess we'll have to find out the hard way, because we are out of time to check. We have to leave, now!"

Hal leapt away from the workstation he'd felt shackled to for hours, even though it had not quite been forty-five minutes. Pris wasn't resisting, but it did seem like he was dragging her along. It took him far longer than it should've to remember her injury and eased up a little.

They surged out into the blinding, late-morning sun. Their exodus briefly slowed while their eyes adjusted, however they knew they had to gain as much distance from the building as possible; every second counted. They were so disoriented they almost ran right into a running police cruiser.

"Maybe that captain isn't so bad after all," Divana said climbing into the driver's seat. She wasted no time testing the vehicle's acceleration limits as they blazed through the broken gate, paying no attention to the fireball behind them where the shiny black cube used to be.

Epilogue: Shooting Stars

Fallout from the ordeal wasn't as extensive as anyone involved expected. Since many of the goings-on were in space, or otherwise unseen with the naked eye, the cover story was a messy combination of a group of hackers and an unexpected meteor shower.

Captain Rufus Wynand of the Riverside County Sheriff's Office made a very convincing statement regarding a crash near Blythe Airfield. At the request of their agencies, Hal and Divana were left out of that report entirely. There were no follow-up calls regarding the property or the three casualties in the crash outside of curious journalists.

Weeks were spent rounding up any remaining people involved in the hostile takeover that could be identified. Akeylah Patel got her wish for an off-world assignment; her and her compatriots were eventually sent to a penal colony on the moon.

Despite being from different agencies, Hal and Divana were not permitted contact with one another during their debriefing, which took several days. During this time, they were asked to repeatedly retrace every move they made, starting with the death of Bredon Fitzroy. This was an old tactic used to break someone down to the point they begin to question themselves, or become so frustrated that converting to being uncooperative seemed like the prudent choice. Both are traps, and Hal caught onto it early in the interview process.

His story cleared by internal security and DOD investigators, Hal now sat in his boss, Anne Kynes's, office going through the same story again, except this time including the part he left out before when he accessed her computer.

"So my name didn't come up at all during the debriefing? Including giving permission to participate in the investigation from the beginning?"

"Only regarding coordinating with Mosin, which we did... eventually. I'm confident he'll verify we met with him, just hopefully not when and where."

Anne sat back contemplatively and said "I don't know if I should be impressed that you followed my instructions to the letter, or disappointed I wasn't more involved. Regardless, it's nice to know I have at least one person I can trust in this office. Having said that, there is a critical need to get the Military Assets and Repurposing Section back up and running, which will require good people to step in and fill a few vacancies. Someone was already appointed as the new supervisor, but I can't think of anyone better to fill Bredon Fitzroy's shoes than you, if you're interested. It's a promotion and doesn't require you to move. What do you say?"

Hal couldn't resist smiling. Anne asked him what the grin was about, and he said "I've kinda been doing the opposite of that most of my career here; *preventing* military equipment from entering civilian usage. Um, I'll have to talk to my wife about it. What's my time limit here?"

"Tough to say. The MARS unit is pretty devastated so there's not much they can do until their ranks are refilled. Shouldn't keep them waiting too long though."

"Copy that boss. Whatever happens I'm eager to get back to work. If you need me, I'll be at my desk."

"One last thing," said Anne. "Have you heard from your friend at the NCIS? Word has it she might be up for promotion as well. Possibly to DC."

"I have heard from her, just not that newsflash. She probably won't consider anything at headquarters a promotion; takes a special type of person to work there."

"Well, potentially saving the world doesn't often go unnoticed. Give her my best, will you?"

Hal nodded and left her office. With a new opportunity looming over him his desk suddenly felt dispiritingly mundane. He was nervous about losing his investigator status, an inspector however came with its own challenges and authorities not wholly different than what he was already doing. Also, the new position may feasibly reduce the circumstances he regularly finds himself in that bring him close to serious injury and death. That would likely be the selling point to Lindsey, so he had to decide whether to lead with that or wait for her to ask about it, along with the more consistent work hours.

Hal's post-military life had largely been as successful as it was because he accepted opportunities when they presented themselves to him; usually in ways he very rarely sought out himself. Why start saying no to providence now?

~

"And you're sure it was destroyed with the building?" Deputy Director Wray Corvo asked for a second time on a video call with Divana Pris.

"Positive sir. The man had to practically drag me out of there because of my gunshot wound. I would've noticed if he grabbed it out of the console right next to me."

"Okay, I believe you. Don't get offended though if I want to personally look at the forensic results from the airstrike wreckage. Changing subjects; have you given any more thought to joining me out here in alphabet city?"

She knew this was coming. Knew it was the main point Wray meant to address, yet she still wasn't prepared for it. "I have sir, and I'm still undecided. The job itself is very tempting, I'm just not sold on the idea of moving my family into the heart of the beast."

"I hear you. DC isn't the easiest place to get excited about. How does splitting your time between east and west coasts sound? Coming out here only a week per month, and when there's serious national security matters?"

Divana furrowed her brow in skepticism. "Was this offer available earlier and I wasn't told or did you make this up on the spot? Doesn't sound like a normal federal arrangement to me."

"Who's to say what's normal in this day and age? This is a brand-new position cobbled together from two others, and frankly I think having a headquarters-level position on the west coast is a good idea; allows us to decentralize somewhat. Plus, people seem to lose their connection to field agents when they come out here for any extended period of time. I want that trend to stop."

"Well, in that case, unless there's some awful catch to all this, I accept those terms sir… with the caveat of withdrawing to my current position if I don't like what I see."

"Making terms already, eh Pris? I'll let you decide if this is a catch or not: your first order of business would be to take a deep look into the Defense Intelligence Agency, particularly regarding their dealings with the Navy and Marine Corps. Recent events have made a lot of people very unhappy around here, which could've been worse if not for the efforts of you and your friend, the good doctor. You'd be teaming up with counterparts with the Air Force's OSI on occasion, but you'll be reporting directly to me, in person. DOD brass wants to do a little more house cleaning on their own terms, rather than the knee-jerk reaction of the past few weeks. NCIS has been tapped to spearhead the operation."

Divana wasn't sure she liked the sound of that, however it was something she agreed needed to be done. "I don't know if I'm the best person for that job, sir. Is there a reason this is being offered to me specifically?"

Deputy Director Corvo leaned forward in his seat and gave her a hard stare. "Because you're one of the few people to have seen Leoben Jardani and lived."

"I'm sorry, who?"

"He goes by the name Jericho in some circles; however, you met him posing as Arkady Mosin."

TO BE CONTINUED...

Other Titles by AJ Blanc:

Pieces of the Whole – 2017

Crossing Rubicon – 2019

The Kadmus Project – 2021

www.ingramcontent.com/pod-product-compliance
Lightning Source LLC
Chambersburg PA
CBHW020322200626
46814CB00006BB/2369

9 7 8 0 9 9 9 4 5 7 4 6 7